T

P9-BEE-803

DATE DUE

DEMCO 38-296

Jake's Orphan

A *Melanie Kroupa* Book

Jake's Orphan

P E G G Y   B R O O K E

DORLING KINDERSLEY PUBLISHING, INC.

A *Melanie Kroupa* Book

Dorling Kindersley Publishing, Inc.
95 Madison Avenue
New York, New York 10016

Visit us on the World Wide Web at http://www.dk.com

*The town of Crosby, North Dakota, is real, and Hawkeye School
was a real school. Everything else in this story is fictional, and resemblances
to real people, living or dead, are purely coincidental.*

Dorling Kindersley books are available at special discounts for bulk purchases for sales
promotions or premiums. Special editions, including personalized covers, excerpts of
existing guides, and corporate imprints can be created in large quantities for specific
needs. For more information, contact Special Markets Dept., Dorling Kindersley
Publishing, Inc., 95 Madison Ave., New York, NY 10016; fax: (800) 600-9098.

Library of Congress Cataloging-in-Publication Data
Brooke, Margaret.
Jake's orphan / by Peggy Brooke.— 1st ed.
p. cm.
Summary: When taken from an orphanage to work on a farm in North Dakota
in 1926, twelve-year-old Tree searches for a home not only for himself but also
for his irrepressible younger brother.
ISBN 0-7894-2628-5
[1. Orphans—Fiction. 2. Brothers—Fiction. 3. Farm life—North Dakota—
Fiction. 4. North Dakota—Fiction.] I. Title.
PZ7.B78975 Jak 2000
[Fic]—dc21
99-046466
Book design by Annemarie Redmond.
The text of this book is set in 13 point Goudy.

Printed and bound in U.S.A.

First Edition, 2000
2 4 6 8 10 9 7 5 3 1

To John, my first, best editor, the one who always believes I can do it. To my mother, who taught me to expect good things always. To my dad, who was a third grader at Hawkeye School in 1926 and a true child and man of the land. To my boys, Justin, Joe, Sam, and Dan, who continue to amaze and inspire me with who they are and what they do.

✳ ✳ ✳

I also want to thank Mary Jack Wald, my agent, who found the right home for Jake's Orphan, and Melanie Kroupa, and her assistant, Sharon McBride, who worked tirelessly with me to bring the book to completion.

Sometimes the flames reached the top of the sky. Great tongues of blue and purple, then red, and later yellow and orange. They crackled and hissed, monster snakes balancing on the tips of their tails, snarling. Long after the roof had burned away, the rafter ribs stood intact, like a deer skeleton I found in the woods once. It was bleached and dry, hard as stone, the skin and muscles rotted down to dust years before. I stared at the blazing rafters until my eyes made out every rib of the silhouette.

The barn went down bellowing like some mad beast. As if its own fury fanned the flames. In the end, when the timbers had collapsed with a sizzling roar that made the earth shudder, after the glowing cinders had spewed up like geysers to the dark, indifferent sky, the whole of it crumbled to a smoldering heap of gray ash that no one would guess had once been a barn. Last of all the hazy outline of my mother's face rose up, ghostlike, with the smoke—and then disappeared.

I woke then, breathing hard, sometimes crying out and waking my bunkmates. I turned my head on the damp pillow to stare out the window, watching for the first pale glimmer in the eastern sky.

One more night had passed.

Hard Bargain

I had no warning the day the Gundersons came. Right after breakfast, just as I was leaving the dining hall for geography class, the breakfast monitor handed me a note to report to the headmaster's office. It didn't say the reason.

"Main thing is we want a hard worker," I heard Mr. Gunderson tell the headmaster as I swung the door open. They all turned at the sound of my boots crossing the wood threshold.

I saw right then that something important was happening.

Neither of the Gundersons smiled as I gave them a nod and walked over to Mr. Blake's desk. "He's a good, willing worker," the headmaster explained, as if to balance off my plain and scrawny looks. I was tall for a twelve-year-old, long legged and gangly. Not much to look at, I knew that. I stood up as straight as

I could while I felt their eyes appraise me, up and down.

"What would you think of sprouting calluses on your hands from farm work?" Mr. Blake prodded me when I didn't think to even say hello.

I nodded eagerly. "I'd like that fine." My voice came out a froggy croak.

Mrs. Gunderson smiled. She was round and soft looking, with little rolls of fat filling her out like a cushioned chair. I smiled back at her.

Her husband frowned. "My name is Gunderson," he said straight out to me. "And this is My Missus." He paused, letting me take in the facts, I guess. I could see he'd been out in the sun and wind a lot; his lean body was dry and wrinkled as a prune. I'd learn later that he was stronger than he looked. "Our own son is grown," he said gruffly, "and we come to find a worker. A boy looking for a roof over his head and food in exchange for long hours of good hard work."

I thought at the time that he was telling me their family story. It turned out he was being fair in his way, giving me a picture of how life would be on their farm.

"He'd go to school," Mr. Blake insisted sternly.

The Gundersons nodded.

"For a year," the headmaster said to me. "Unless they decide they'll adopt you."

I swallowed hard. "My brother?" I asked hoarsely while Mr. Blake's eyes were still fastened on mine. I figured I had nothing to lose by asking.

He turned back to the Gundersons. "He has a brother. Two years younger. Could you consider taking both?"

The Gundersons exchanged glances. They could speak that way; something with their eyes, the lift of the brow or the set of the jaw, I can't say. But they understood each other clear as day.

"There's just room for one," Gunderson answered in a moment. I watched his Missus, and sure enough, she slid her eyes right past mine down to the floor with a little disappointed set to her lips. As though he'd read her right, and then decided himself.

Their offer came to me like a sudden shift of wind. I'd hoped so long and wished so hard that someday someone would come and pick me out that all I could feel was a heady kind of excitement building, clouding my brain. I couldn't even think what it would mean, leaving my brother.

"We'll want to be headin' out on the train this

afternoon. We'll take him with us now so we can do some shopping before we leave. How soon can he be ready?"

Mr. Blake fastened his eyes on mine. "I'll have Tillie get you a duffel to pack your things," he said. "I'll find your brother and let him know you're leaving and send him up to your room."

Those words hit me like a splash of cold water. I was leaving the orphanage at last, the place where my brother and I had turned up when I was only three. After the fire. After our mother died. Now I'd be going back to the wide world I'd always believed would open for me someday—the day my life would begin again. But I'd be going on my own.

Mr. Blake seemed to think it would work out all right. Still, as I trudged down the worn steps and across the yard, my boots felt heavy and so did my heart. It was the summer of 1926, and the St. Paul Orphanage was no better or worse than most places for homeless boys, I suppose. Four long buildings stood along the outside edges of the grounds, un-painted and stained gray by the weather. A few scat-tered tufts of grass had survived the boot scuffs of several hundred boys over the years, but mostly the yard was packed dirt that turned to mud when it rained and washed down the hill to the dairy and gardens that we tended all summer long.

I shared a dormitory room with ten boys my age. It was quiet now with all of them in class. I unbuckled the straps of the stiff black duffel bag, feeling torn in two. As if some great power had struck a cruel bargain with me, flung open the doors to let me escape but locked my brother in. Making me a traitor for doing the very thing I'd set my hopes on as long as I could remember. I'd never planned it this way, but then an orphan hasn't much opportunity to make plans. Dreams, maybe. Hopes. Plenty of those.

I stuffed my spare pair of pants in the bag.

"You really goin', then?" I jumped at the sound of Acorn's voice. It was always deeper than you'd expect from a little kid. His hair was straight and brown, like mine only lighter. His face was freckled, not neatly sprinkled but in deep brown blotches that looked like he'd stood too close to a muddy road when a buggy clattered by. He smiled in that winsome way he had that always tugged at me.

I looked away. "Got a chance to work for a farmer," I said, glancing around to see what else I ought to take. My bed was just like all the others, a black iron frame with a lumpy mattress thrown over saggy springs. The bedding belonged to the orphanage. The little table did, too. I picked up my comb. I'd already taken my oversize coat and a shirt from the hook on the wall. There wasn't much to pack.

"I'll take this," I said gruffly, pulling a wooden-handled hunting knife from under my mattress and showing it to Acorn.

His eyes bugged out at the sight of it, and then he grinned. "*You* saved my hide!" he exclaimed, surprised and pleased.

I mustered a little smile as I considered where I ought to stow the knife. I couldn't let myself think what kind of scrapes Acorn would get himself into without me to rescue him. "You thought it just disappeared into thin air?"

The knife had returned with Acorn after one of his late-night adventures. My brother was quick-tempered and just as quick with his fists. Even more worrisome was his talent for slipping out of windows or doors carelessly left unlocked after the last light was turned off at night. Don't get me wrong, I had no love for the orphanage; but Acorn had a sort of burning resentment of the place, as though it was some monster that threatened to devour him. I couldn't count the number of times he had disappeared.

He always came back. Whether from cold or

hunger or loneliness, I never could tell. Then, every couple of weeks, he slipped out again. Sometimes he was caught, sometimes not. It didn't matter. Barred windows only meant Acorn had to sneak a little farther afield, to find windows unbarred on a higher floor. Locks only meant he had to pilfer a wire from somewhere and feel his way around in the keyhole. Acorn had no fear of heights, maybe no fear of anything. Tree branches were like arms reaching up to catch him, and he could shinny down a rainspout as if he were part monkey.

Acorn liked to go out along the railroad tracks and hang out with bums who huddled around their fires in the woods. One night he stumbled across a hobo sprawled unconscious on the tracks. Hearing the sound of a train whistle, Acorn scrambled to find the other hoboes to help him roll and drag the fellow to safety. The next time Acorn sneaked out, the man rewarded his heroism by giving him his knife, a prized possession for a man living out on the land. At least, that's how Acorn told the story later that night when he came back with the knife stuffed inside his shirt.

All seemed well until a week or so later, when that same hobo was caught loitering around a St. Paul bank the day it was robbed. The police questioned him, pressing him to admit he'd hidden the stolen money somewhere. He must have been desperate enough to forget his gratefulness, because he quickly concocted a tale about an orphan boy he'd seen running off with what looked like a sack of money. "That kid was a foxy one," the man declared. "He's the same one lifted my knife." The hobo had lots of friends who could identify the unusual carvings on the knife handle. "I carved it myself," he told the police. "Dressed it up with moons and stars. There's not another like it."

I was mopping the floor outside Mr. Blake's office when the police chief came to tell him the hobo's story. I knew right away they were talking about Acorn's knife. I also knew the first orphan Mr. Blake would suspect would be my brother.

Quiet as a cat, I stashed the mop and bucket in the hall closet and slipped away to Acorn's bunk. I found the knife under his mattress and stuffed it inside my own shirt before creeping back around behind the shoe shop to resume my mopping. I'd never told Acorn I'd taken the knife—I'd hoped he'd worry about it some and maybe change his ways.

"I thought . . . I thought I got a guardian angel," Acorn said now as he watched me slip the knife deep into the pants leg inside my bag. "Thought maybe it had a magic blade and *poof!*—it disappeared!" Acorn's pale face lit up, and his brown eyes sparkled like they did when he told me about his nighttime adventures. "Should of known it was you," he finished, his voice suddenly husky.

I buckled the black bag shut, trying to think what to say. "I didn't want anybody guessing where it went," I mumbled, finally.

"It was useless without some way to keep the blade sharp anyhow."

I glanced uneasily at Acorn, wondering for the hundredth time what use he had planned for the knife. That was the most worrisome thing about Acorn. You never knew what he'd think up next.

I drew a breath and made myself focus on leaving. I didn't know how to say good-byes. People slipped away without more than a "S'long" at the orphanage. Still, it seemed like something more should be said to a brother. "This fellow's farm is in North Dakota," I said. "It sounds like it's a fair piece off. Be gone a year. Unless he adopts me. He does that, I'll send for you."

"A year?" Acorn echoed. His eyes were wide and unblinking, planted on my face.

I sat on the bed so my gaze was level with his. "They can keep me for a year," I explained carefully. "If they don't adopt me, they have to send me back." I was already figuring that I could work hard enough to make the Gundersons want my brother, too. "I'll write," I told him confidently, suddenly seeing how simple it would be. "As soon as the Gundersons say it's all right for you to come, I'll send a letter."

Acorn licked his lips and swallowed. That heavy-hearted feeling came over me again, and I quickly turned away and stood up to go. "They've only got room for one," I told him. "For now, that is."

"I'm going to follow you to the train station," Acorn said suddenly. "My buddies out in the woods told me all about hoppin' a train."

"What do you mean, follow me?" I demanded, sounding gruffer than I felt. I glanced at the door to be sure no one was listening. "I'm leaving with the Gundersons right away. They've got a buggy. You'd never keep up with us, Acorn, even if you didn't get caught running off."

My brother stared at me, frowning. Then he squared his shoulders. "What time does the train leave?" he asked. "I'll wait till dinner, when nobody's watchin'. I know where the tracks are, and I'll catch it as it swings by."

"No, Acorn," I said as stern as I could, thinking in a rising panic that Acorn would ruin everything—and I didn't know how to make him understand I *had* to go, for both of us. "You'd never find the right train; there's tracks leading everywhere from St. Paul. You can't . . . You'll only get lost and end up in deep trouble." I was pleading now, losing patience that he was being so stubborn, and feeling scared and sorry, all at once. "Listen, Acorn. You can't come along. You have to wait here for me. I *promise*—if I don't come back I'll send for you. Give me your word you won't sneak out while I'm gone."

Acorn raked my face with those burning brown eyes, his jaw set. It was clear he thought I had no business laying down the law, especially now when he figured I was deserting him.

"You've got to stay here and stay out of trouble, Acorn. A year's not so long, really." I said that, knowing full well a year was forever and then some when you're ten and your only brother is leaving you behind.

Acorn's eyes scanned my face and then, to my relief, seemed to soften a little. He shrugged, backing up a step as if this good-bye had taken long enough.

I bit my lip and picked up my duffel. Acorn didn't give up easily, I knew that. "Don't try to follow me," I said again, firmer, thinking if I acted sure and solid he'd understand it was the right thing that I was doing. "I told you before, as soon as I can, I'll send for you. You've got my word—now give me yours."

Acorn looked at the floor. "I'll watch for your let-ter," he mumbled.

He sounded so far away already that I wanted to stop right there and tell him everything all over. *Make* him see. *Make* him promise me he'd wait for my letter. But the Gundersons were waiting; I heard Mr. Blake call and knew I was out of time.

I turned back at the door. "S'long," I said.

Acorn stiffened his fingers and touched them to his forehead in a mock salute before he plopped down on the edge of my bed and watched me go.

I left him there, one leg curled under him on the sagging mattress and the other dangling carelessly over the side. I knew there was nothing careless about what he was thinking. Even though he was my brother, I'd never understood all that burned inside him. Still, he'd said he'd watch for the letter; he'd given me that much. So I figured he'd have to stay until he heard from me. My brother wasn't a liar. That, I told myself, I could count on.

Untamed Country

We boarded the train late in the afternoon. I knew from a map on the wall in the station that we'd be heading north and west. We were still chugging along in the morning, and I woke up relieved that at least this night I hadn't dreamed of the fire and my mother's face. While we ate Mrs. Gunderson's cold pancakes and butter and jam, I stared at the fast-passing North Dakota prairie. The wind blew the grass in endless ripples of green, clear out to where it touched the rim of the sprawling dome of sky.

Mostly I saw pictures in my mind. Memories of my days at the orphanage, days I never dared believe would finally end. I remembered the time I was roughed up by a tall boy we called Bean and the time the schoolmaster had me hold out my hands so he could crop them with the ruler because I'd flunked the spelling test. It was the morning after Acorn had sneaked out to go sliding on a nearby pond with some of his pals. He'd fallen through the ice and plunged into cold water. His friends couldn't reach him, but somehow he held on until Mr. Blake arrived with a rope and pulled him out.

I couldn't sleep that night from worrying. After the lights were out, I crept down to the infirmary and huddled in a ball at the foot of Acorn's bed. Just listening to his breathing, hard and raspy as it was, helped me keep calm. It was easy enough to hide in the shadows when the nurse came to check him, but I crept away before morning, not wanting to risk getting in trouble.

The next day my spelling words were just a blur on the paper. My eyes wouldn't even focus. The punishment didn't matter. All that mattered was that Acorn was all right.

Now, as the train rumbled on, I chewed Mrs. Gunderson's pancakes, half watching the grass rippling under the wind fingers and thinking of the look on my brother's face when I'd left. I was glad I hadn't told him the Gundersons didn't want him, and sorry at the same time that I hadn't said I'd spoken up for him in Mr. Blake's office. The rhythm of the swaying train, the clack-clack of wheels on rails, kept my mind turning round and round, trying to think what I could have done different, what I could have said different to make the Gundersons say Acorn could come, too.

The truth was, over and over I wondered if the right thing would have been for me to stay.

The Missus handed me a jar of cider to wash down the pancakes. I took a quick sip, feeling Mr. Gunderson's eyes on me, as if he was watching to see if I'd gulp more than my share. The cider was as sharp as vinegar and warm from sitting in Mrs. Gunderson's basket on the hot train. I held it out to him, but he didn't show a sign he'd even seen it, just kept his eyes on my face. His wife took the jar and turned the lid down tight with her plump fingers.

"How many cows you milked?" Mr. Gunderson asked abruptly.

I started to answer but had to clear my throat. "I just . . . I just learned to milk this summer," I said. "I had my own cow every day."

"Just one?" His tone was sharp.

"Yes, sir." I felt myself turning red. It was only the last few weeks I'd been able to finish even that one cow without Mr. Madden, the dairyman, sending one of the older, experienced boys to finish her off.

"Done any haying?"

"No, sir."

He shot his wife an exasperated glare. "That Blake fellow didn't want to part with his good workers," he grunted. Then, to me, "He told me he hated to lose you just when you're finally getting old enough to be a real help. Looks like it'll work out good for him if we teach you farmin' and then send you back next year all trained."

I wasn't sure if I was supposed to answer. I ducked my head and bit off a sliver of pancake even though I'd lost my appetite. He'd cleared up any questions I'd had about why I'd been chosen.

Mr. Gunderson studied me a few more minutes before he suddenly clapped his hat on his head and pulled himself up. He stood there a moment, looming over me, swaying with the train. "It's stuffy as hell in here. I'm going to get some air," he growled.

I watched him amble unsteadily down the aisle, out of step with the rocking train. As he pulled open the car door and let it whoosh shut behind him, my mind turned stubbornly back to the many times I'd seen other boys leave the orphanage—all the times I'd tried to figure out what made them different, what made them stand out from the rest enough to be picked. I'd come to think of myself as gray and color-less, just like the orphanage. There was a sameness to the days there, always hunger, always too cold in win-

ter and too hot in summer. And there was a sameness
to us boys, except for a few remarkable fellows like
Bean and the one we called Red because his hands
and face were a flaming color and because he bossed
us around. It fit him. The color fit. He stood out that
way from our grayness.

We all had real names, but they were locked up in
files along with our pasts. My brother and I shared a
name, Smith, but we never used it. The name didn't
mean a thing to us. It was as if on that fiery night our
mother had left us only that one key—without even a
clue to what it could unlock.

Sometimes we boys strapped each other with make-
shift names that fit more or less like our secondhand
clothes. We wore them like overalls that could be
shed when they were outgrown. They tied us to nothing. Real names, as close as I could figure, were meant
to be a link to one's beginnings.

Tree was the name my brother gave me. That was
my shape to him, I guess, maybe from my wild hair
sprouting out the top. Or maybe it was my size compared to his, looking up. He never said. I learned in
third grade that acorns are tree seeds, so the next time
we had a talk, I called him that. I tried to explain its
meaning, but Acorn had no time for long explana-
tions, or even short ones. I don't think he stopped to

wonder what the name meant at all. He liked the sound all right, and that was good enough for him.

* * *

By late afternoon the familiar long grass of Minnesota had shortened down to wheatgrass, as Mr. Gunderson called it. Wildflowers bobbed their heads at the passing train. I saw a curious gopher rear up on his haunches to watch us steam by just as a hawk swooped down to clasp him in his talons. He spread his wide wings and flew away, clutching his wiggling prey.

"Sure a lot of wide open space," I said, wondering at a land that trees don't naturally take to.

"Lots of fresh air," Mr. Gunderson agreed, with a kind of pride in his voice. "And nothin' blockin' the view."

We jolted on and on, stopping at every depot along the tracks. Another night passed and another day before we finally wheeled into the little station in Crosby. We were about as far west as we could go in North Dakota, six hundred miles from St. Paul. I counted five grain elevators looming over the town and a shiny new water tower that stood like a giant on stilts with CROSBY proudly painted on its side.

We snatched up our bags and scrambled out of

the passenger car and down the metal steps. Mr. Gunderson led us in a weaving line between the buggies and motorcars clustered around the depot.

"This here's Jake," Mr. Gunderson said as he threw his bag into the back of a wagon. I looked up into a pair of sky blue eyes. They flicked over my skinny frame and seemed to take in all of me in one glance. I wondered what they saw.

"This here's the orphan," Mr. Gunderson explained as Jake looped the reins over the brake stick and jumped down from the wagon seat. It was a light spring wagon, a two-seater loaded with a box of groceries, two sacks of flour, and an empty cream can.

Jake shook my hand. His grip was rough, but warm. He was slim like Mr. Gunderson but taller and smoother cheeked. I knew they were brothers without being told. They seemed alike, just weathered differently, like the north and south sides of the same deep-rooted tree. Jake wore no cap and his head was bald, a creamy burnished leather. A fringe of soft brown fuzz grew from ear to ear around the back of his head. Altogether it looked as if the top of his head was a beefy mushroom grown right up through the half circle of his hair. I felt an urge to touch it just to feel its spongy warmth.

Mr. Gunderson tossed our things quickly into the

wagon, shoving the cream can forward under the backseat to make room and motioning for me to climb in. Then he helped the Missus hoist her stout legs over the wheel. Jake scrambled in last and picked up the reins.

"Too bad you ain't learned to drive the flivver," Mr. Gunderson remarked to Jake as we lumbered past the domed courthouse and the row of cars parked on the main street. There was a tall hotel just across from the courthouse lawn. I counted three banks and a dozen painted storefronts before I gave it up. Overalled farmers and mothers with shrieking children bustled and jostled here and there on the broad wooden sidewalks.

Jake gave an expert flick to the reins. "Horses are a lot easier to talk to than cars," he replied. He turned over his shoulder as he answered and gave me a little wink. I took a deep breath, suddenly feeling like the warm air was carrying all the new sights and sounds deep into my veins.

Just south of town, we skirted a broad, swampy place they called a slough. We turned east, then south, mounting a little rise where we could see the countryside sprawled before us. It made me think of a rolling crazy quilt, the fields and pastures different shades of brown and dark green, like old cloth that had been rough cut and pieced together without a thought to design. Here and there a small cluster of farm buildings huddled, puny and plain under the high, wide sky.

"Look at Ferguson's barn," Mr. Gunderson remarked to Jake, pointing off to the left. I studied the building, remembering the flaming barns I'd seen in my dreams. It had a hole in the roof, with charred rafters jutting through. Mr. Gunderson swung his thin shoulders around to study it as we passed. "Oddest thing, lightning hittin' like it did and then rain dousing the fire before it burned the whole thing."

The barn had no door, only an opening where one should have been, and the windowpanes were mostly broken. It stood empty, abandoned. Gray and plain.

"Looks like Ferguson ought to tear it down before it falls over," he declared.

"I heard Ferguson sold it," Jake drawled. "Ole Oleson thinks he can move it to his place and fix it up. Says he thinks it's still solid."

Mr. Gunderson raised his bushy eyebrows, then swooped them down in a dark frown. "Sounds like a lot of work to me. I wonder what kind of money old Ferguson made him dig up for that heap of used firewood."

I didn't hear Jake's reply. I was craning my neck to

look back, feeling glad that somebody planned to nail the door back up and repair the glass panes before the wind and snow blew in and wrecked it worse. With the roof gouged away, the barn looked like something had reached down and torn out the insides—like the heart, maybe, had been ripped out by some mighty power. A shiver rippled down my spine, making me feel as though somehow I'd been given a warning. As if a voiceless something spoke deep inside me, making me see for the first time a new picture of the orphanage—as hard as I'd set my heart on escaping it, the St. Paul Orphanage for Homeless Boys had been, after all, a very safe place to be.

No Turning Back

The first thing I saw was the windmill, standing like a sentinel over the Gundersons' farm. The blades quietly whirled while the tail danced freely to the east and then the southeast, steered by the invisible breath of the wind.

Mr. Gunderson noticed me leaning way back to study it. "Say hello to the prairie wind," he grimaced, glancing up himself. "It never rests." And then, almost under his breath, "It's got more power than God."

There was that pride in his voice again. *Bigger* than God, that's what he meant. It made me understand better how worthless I sounded when I said I'd only milked one cow. Mr. Gunderson measured me—I guess he measured even God—against a mighty long rod.

I sighed and let my eyes slide back down the tower and wander around the farm. The Gundersons' barn was taller and broader than the house and in need of paint, especially on the south side, where the sun had had her way. Set back a little was a chicken coop, and on the other side were two more small buildings. One had a wide door and might house the flivver Mr. Gunderson had mentioned. The other was a little shanty with a window, Jake's house they said it was. Five rows of scrawny trees edged three sides of the farm. "Shelter belt," Mr. Gunderson called them. But they weren't any kind of shelter yet. They were short, not even as tall as the clothesline. The farm seemed open, defenseless against the sun and wind.

The main house stood by itself, white, two stories tall, with a pillared porch on the front. Chickens scratched and pecked in the yard as we drove up.

Mrs. Gunderson took me right upstairs to show me where to put my things. "This is Gus's old room," she said, swinging open the door and stepping back to let me through. The heat of August, all bottled up in the room, closed over me when I walked in. Dust motes danced in the light from the window. I set my duffel bag on the wooden-framed bed. It was a strange feeling, one that would take some getting used to—my own room; my own window looking out. There was a white flour-sack curtain and a round rag rug on the floor right where a person would swing his feet out of bed in the morning. Even the brown floorboards seemed smoother than those at the orphanage.

Mrs. Gunderson made a clucking noise with her tongue and scurried over to pry up the inside window. "Gets so hot in here!" she fussed. "And these windows! I washed everything, but the dust is always coming in. You maybe don't have such dust in Minnesota." I realized she was apologizing to me. "It's very nice," I said. I came up beside her and followed her gaze out the window, staring down on the brave little trees and the pasture rolling off till it butted up against the sky. I could see the water tower and grain elevators standing like fat little men on the horizon. "Nothing blocking the view," I said.

Mrs. Gunderson looked at me sharply. She'd propped open a little hinged stick to let in three finger-holes of air below the outside glass pane. I held my fingertips in front of them to feel the air moving. "Don't know if it's hotter inside or out," she sighed. Then she walked heavily back to the door. "Put your things in the closet. Then go on out to the barn."

✳ ✳ ✳

The cows were coming in for milking as I got there. The first two rolled their eyes at me, startled, but at a grunt from Mr. Gunderson they silently ambled their way to their own places.

Jake bent to pick up two feed pails. "Come," he said to me. I followed him to the bin of ground oats. We filled the pails and walked down the two rows of cows, plumping oats into the bare-wood mangers where their heads poked through the stanchions. I liked the barn. It was plain and cozy and smelled the way cows do, earthy and fresh breathed and warm.

Mr. Gunderson didn't even look up from his milking as Jake produced a little three-legged wooden stool from the shadows and gestured for me to bring a tin pail and start in.

I sat down and set the bucket between my knees, reminding myself of everything Mr. Madden had taught us. My hand shook a little as I slid my fingers gently down each teat to make the cow let down her milk. Then I started pulling as steady as I could. "Keep it easy now," Jake said quietly before he went to start on the cow behind me.

I could hear the milk splatting in a rhythmic clamor in the bottom of Jake's bucket. In a few minutes the sound quieted to a foaming swish-swish as the liquid rose higher in his pail. My cow's milk came out in harsh, irregular spurts that jangled loud against the tin. I tried to work faster, pulling and squeezing until my wrist and fingers ached.

Mr. Gunderson finished his first cow and came around to watch my struggle. "You're stiff," he stated grimly. "Your wrists are too tight. Loosen up." I tried harder than ever, willing my aching fingers to relax yet somehow keep pumping. "Humph," he mumbled.

Later, when the two of them were done, Mr. Gunderson appeared again. This time he bent over, peering into my half-filled bucket, his mouth set in a tight line. "I'll finish," he grunted, nudging me off my stool with his knee. "You go see if you can learn how to run the cream separator." I knew he was thinking Mr. Blake must have sent him the slowest milker in the whole orphanage.

I followed Jake into the cool, dark separator room. First he lit a lantern and set it on a niche in the stone wall. Then, lifting his bucket, he poured milk into the bowl at the top of the machine. I grasped the crank and started turning, first with one hand, and then, when my arm was tired, with the other. The separator hummed a high little tune as it spun, sending the pale skim milk out the lower spout while the higher one meted out the thick, yellowish cream.

The sun was setting fire to the western sky when we finally turned the cows out and lugged our full cream pails to the house. We left the skim milk for the calves and chickens, and Mr. Gunderson carried a pail of whole milk for the kitchen. Jake opened a slanted trapdoor just outside the kitchen window, and we carried the cream down into the cellar before we went inside for supper.

Mrs. Gunderson had the table all ready when we came in. She smiled at me and turned to set out a platter of ground hash, a great mound of it, and a bowl of thick brown gravy. There were green peas and carrots alongside a sliced loaf of bread. I had never seen so much food—and for only four people!

Mrs. Gunderson clasped her hands over her empty plate and said a little prayer before we dished up and dug in. No one remarked on the meal, as if it was an ordinary thing. No one talked at all. I thought to myself, if this was how people ate in North Dakota, it was sure some country to be living in.

Mr. Gunderson reached out to help himself to more hash and gravy and handed them on to me. As I scooped a second helping, I thought how Acorn's eyes would pop at the sight of all this food. That thought made my stomach tighten up. Acorn would be eating his bread and potatoes and beans about now—every last bite—and he'd still be hungry. If only he'd come, too. If only I'd somehow brought him with me. But even as I thought it, part of me wondered how he'd ever manage here—Mr. Gunderson would have no patience at all with someone as noisy and full of questions as Acorn.

I was sopping the last of my gravy on a thick slice of bread when Mrs. Gunderson jumped up from the table. She thrust a chipped enamel basin in the dry sink, filled it with steaming water from a kettle on the stove, and went to work, washing dishes as if the survival of the world depended on it. It seemed a wonder that the little painted flowers on the plates weren't scuffed clean away.

"Take a towel there and dry those dishes for the Missus," Mr. Gunderson ordered. I shoved back my plate and scrambled to do what he said.

"I want you and the boy to finish binding the wheat while I go to work with John Whitcomb's crew," he told Jake, leaning back in his chair and stretching his legs comfortably.

"Yep. We can handle it," Jake agreed. "Could be the crew got to Sutter's by now. If the weather holds they could be here by the end of next week."

"I'll take Joe and Jen over there first thing in the morning," Mr. Gunderson said. "John told me he could use another team for haulin' bundles. He pays fair. Might as well be helpin' 'em get here sooner."

Mrs. Gunderson handed me another cup to dry. The warmth of the kitchen was making my eyes feel heavy. I blinked hard, forcing them to focus on the cup in my hands.

Mr. Gunderson lit up a pipe. "You keep this boy busy workin' with you," he said to Jake.

"Yep." Jake nodded. "We'll get the harness ready. Wagon wheels need grease."

"And if Jake runs out of jobs for the boy, you find him something to do," Mr. Gunderson said over his shoulder to his wife. "He can help dig potatoes or do what garden gatherin' you need for the cook car."

Mrs. Gunderson nodded, scrubbing away at a roasting pan.

When we'd finished the dishes the Missus sent me out to the privy. "We'll get that bed made up in Gus's room," she said.

"Who's Gus?" I asked later as I helped her tug the sheets smooth on the bed.

"Gus is our son," she replied without looking up. "Did you notice his picture in the hallway when you came up?"

I remembered the picture. Gus was a thin-faced

young man who looked about as sad as anyone I'd ever seen.

"Where is he now?" I asked, hoping I wasn't being rude.

"Gus has gone to Fargo to work in banking with his uncle," she replied curtly. "Now, you hush your questions and get some sleep. Morning comes early. You and Jake and I will have to do the milking when Delton leaves for the threshing crew."

I wondered how Mrs. Gunderson would fit her broad behind on the little milking stool and what she would say about how slowly I milked. But I was too tired to ponder long. My eyelids closed before she even shut the door.

Still, I couldn't sleep. Her steps going downstairs woke me as soon as I dozed off and for a moment I thought it was Acorn coming. I started to drift off once more, but soon voices in the kitchen woke me again.

". . . it's not just that he's puny," Mr. Gunderson was saying, "he's slow. I'll bet he don't know the first thing about horses."

"But Mr. Blake said he was smart. And he seems eager to please," Mrs. Gunderson countered.

"I hate timidity in a boy. He doesn't look strong. I should have insisted he give me someone older."

I rubbed my eyes and rolled over to hear better. Their voices floated clearly through the floor grate where the light from the kitchen filtered through, painting wispy shadows on the wall.

Mrs. Gunderson sighed. "It takes time for a boy to learn."

"Time!" Mr. Gunderson snorted as if the very thought irritated him.

"Yes. Well, we discussed this before."

"I don't know how wise it was to fetch him here. A city boy. It won't bring Gus back, you know."

"I'm not looking to replace Gus any more than you are. Don't worry, Delton, I don't want another son to love and lose."

"A son to lose!" His voice cracked with bitterness. "You blame me, don't you, that Gus left like he did."

"I never said that, Delton."

"You never said! You didn't have to say! You saddle me with guilt—just by lookin' at me."

She sighed again, deeper. "His heart was never strong—"

"And you were always so quick to jump in and make sure he wouldn't get overtired!"

"Me! Only because you were so determined to get all the work you could out of him!" she cried, as if she'd been wounded.

A sharp silence followed her outburst. Then a chair scraped and I heard his boots tread heavily across the floor.

"We shouldn't have brought the orphan here if it brings all this back, Etta," Mr. Gunderson said, his voice gentler but firm.

She didn't speak. There was only a little soft sound as if perhaps she was crying.

I lay waiting for her answer, but it never came. After a while I heard his boots on the floor again, and then there was silence.

It seemed a long time before the light downstairs was shut off and my room snuffed into darkness. The moonlight slowly asserted itself, and I could make out the two doors—like giants towering angrily over me. It was a good thing I wasn't a little kid. The closet door was slightly open, and for a second I thought about grabbing my things and running away. It was an odd thought, one I'd expect Acorn to have.

Remembering my brother, I felt an aching, as though there was a hollow, empty spot inside me, and I wondered for a moment if the whole trip might have been a dream and I would wake up in the morning and find myself whisked back on those shining steel rails past all the little depots to St. Paul.

I wondered what Acorn was thinking, if he was

remembering my promise or if he was asleep by now. Maybe he was awake, swallowing down lonely tears. Then I remembered this was the third night since I'd left him. Acorn would have cried, if he let himself cry, the first night. But by now he'd have steeled himself to go on. In fact, the more I thought about it, picturing the wide, empty look in his eyes when I'd told him that a year wasn't all that long, I was sure he hadn't let himself cry even the first night.

On an impulse I sprang from the bed and tiptoed to the closet. I swung the door back, hoping no one downstairs heard its tired creak, and felt around on the floor under the hook where I'd looped my pants. My fingers found the stiff edge of the duffel bag, and I threw back the top flap and felt inside. The knife was there, solid and cold.

I smiled to myself. The knife seemed like a link between my brother and me, something to hold onto for the year that stretched ahead. I wished I'd thought to say it like that to Acorn—a way to make him think of my keeping his treasure as a bond between us.

The solid weight of the heavy blade grounded me back to the moment. The Gundersons were real, and the cows and the barn, and all those endless miles of prairie we'd crossed. I was finally where I'd always wanted to be—in a real home.

I silently tucked the knife back in my bag, in a way placing my lonely, jumbled thoughts of Acorn there, too.

When I stood up, I stood facing forward, determined I would somehow find a way to become a real son to the Gundersons. Gus was gone. Surely I could work hard enough to change their thinking and make them so glad they'd taken me in that they'd want to adopt me as their new son.

And then—it only made sense—they'd change their minds about Acorn, too.

Tough Man to Please

L ong before sunup, I heard the clop-clop of horses' hooves and the jingle of harness as Mr. Gunderson drove Joe and Jen out of the yard. I drifted back to sleep and didn't wake up until Mrs. Gunderson called me at what must have been first light. I smelled ham sizzling as I scrambled into my clothes.

"Mornin'," Jake said, nodding to me from a chair by the kitchen table. Mrs. Gunderson was just handing him his plate as I passed on my way to the outhouse.

"Mornin'." I nodded back. The early-rising chickens looked up and took a few steps forward when I went out on the porch. As soon as I started down the steps, they fell back to pecking in the dirt, disappointed it was only me.

The sky was a blaze of rose and peach and gold streamers high above the land. Birds twittered their morning calls back and forth. The wind was awake, too, the only force that seemed to take notice of me, tickling my ears and fingering my face and hair like a blind man learning my features by touch.

"Hello, wind," I whispered.

* * *

Jake and I went to let in the cows while Mrs. Gunderson put things away in the kitchen. It was quiet and comfortable being with Jake. His eyes had a friendly sparkle for me as he crooned a soft, "Come, Baw-ss," to the cows.

"They all named Boss?" I asked him as we stood waiting for the cows to come up to the door.

Jake laughed. "They all come if you call 'em just about anything. Some have names. There's Dolly with the white diamond face," he showed me, pointing. "That one's Belle. There's Bess. And Rosie. Guess the ones we've had the longest have a name attached."

"Could I name the others?"

Jake's eyes skimmed thoughtfully over me. "You do that," he said. "It's past time we got the rest of them named."

"You two seem to be enjoying yourselves." Mrs. Gunderson smiled at me as she came up behind us from the front of the barn. She'd wrapped her hair in a flowered cotton scarf pulled low, almost to her eyebrows, and tied in a fat knot at the back of her neck. "Is this Bess?" I asked Jake as the cows filed in. "And that Dolly?" I wanted to be sure I remembered them right. Mrs. Gunderson shook her head, but her eyes twinkled, as Jake started down the row, closing their stanchions, reciting the names again. When the Missus walked over to pick up a bucket, I remembered to scramble for the feed pail and put out the oats.

All the time we milked, I thought about names. Girls' names, they ought to be, but I didn't know very many. One of the cows had sad-looking eyes, so I could call her Sad Eyes. And the one with the narrow face and pink nose . . . what about Pretty Face? I got the idea I could make them each a sign, maybe, to mark their place. It felt like the right thing to do, considering they were smart enough to find their own spot every time they came in.

Jake finished milking his cows before I was done with Rosie. He tapped my shoulder, motioning me to go on and start the cream separator while he squeezed out the last of Rosie's milk. My aching fingers were glad for the change. I liked the feel of knowing a job without being told what to do, even if my shoulders and back kicked up a fuss. Everything was sort of easy without Mr. Gunderson around. We all worked hard, but . . . more peaceably.

Jake and I turned the cows out to pasture when the milking was done. I helped him get the harness on Babe and Black and a younger, chestnut team named Pet and Pal. We walked them out to the field where the binder was waiting, the sun warm on our backs. Even the dust seemed friendly as it puffed at our heels.

After we'd hitched up the horses, Jake climbed onto the seat and clucked for them to start. The binder reel revolved in a wide circle, sweeping the wheat stalks toward the cutter bar. As I walked along-side him, Jake showed me how to run the foot pedal to throw off the bundles. "You try it now," he said, whoa-ing the horses and jumping down.

I scrabbled up, scared and excited. Jake walked along, encouraging me with quiet instructions. Gradually I found an easy rhythm to driving the horses and running the foot pedal and I relaxed, proud to be learning another job. Later, we let the horses rest and stacked the fallen bundles into shocks.

The next day we finished the binding and rolled up the canvas before we went to work oiling and re-pairing harness. We greased wagon wheels and set up an elevator Jake had built to load the grain into bins. Through it all, through the milking and a hundred other chores, there was the easy feeling of working together and making everything ready. I wished Acorn was here. Wished I could hear him brag up Mrs. Gunderson's cooking and see his eyes at the sight of the food on her table. I wished he could feel as strong and smart as I did with all I was learning.

"Mr. Gunderson will sure be pleased with all we've got done," I remarked one bright afternoon as the Missus, Jake, and I jolted along the road to town. We needed groceries, and there were eggs to sell and butter and cream to deliver.

They both glanced at me, as though I'd said something surprising. Mrs. Gunderson gave me a quick little smile before she looked away across the fields again.

"Yep, he'll be here any time now," Jake replied. His words, not really an answer, hit me like a splash of icy water on our sunny day. I felt I'd got it wrong again—that just because I was pleased didn't mean Mr. Gunderson would feel the same. The wind picked up then, almost as if it, too, disapproved, and whisked my childish words away.

The next evening at supper time, Mr. Gunderson drove Joe and Jen into the yard and announced that the threshers would be here in the morning. "You plan to be up early, boy," he directed as he reached for another helping of potatoes. "Threshing time, everybody's got to be up before the sun. Come down to the barn to curry horses and give 'em some oats as soon as the Missus calls." Then to Jake, "We'll load a wagon of oats tonight. I'll take it out to the field first thing in the morning."

Jake nodded.

Mr. Gunderson glanced again at me. "We got to keep a whole threshing crew of horses fed," he said with a frown. "So I'll get the oats there at sunup. You'll help Jake get the milkin' done before you come out to the field. Then you find me and I'll give you a job."

I nodded, swallowing hard.

"I hate the thought of leavin' a team of horses here in the pasture," Mr. Gunderson grumbled. "Just couldn't find another wagon this year."

"We might be glad to have a fresh team later," Jake replied calmly.

I reminded myself I'd done fine while Mr. Gunderson was gone—I could finish milking Rosie all by myself now, and Jake had been pleased with how I handled a team. Still, I knew it was Mr. Gunderson's opinion that mattered. I hadn't proved a thing to him yet.

I wondered if I could.

44

* * *

Even before Jake and I let the cows in, I heard the threshing wagons creaking into the oat field in the morning. The two of us hurried through the milking, me almost finishing a second cow before Jake was done with the others. Then we hitched Babe and Black to a wagon that we'd loaded with baskets of potatoes for the cook car. I couldn't wait to get out to the field and see the crew in action. At the same time, I wondered what job Mr. Gunderson had planned for me. I hoped I could do it good enough.

John Whitcomb rode over to meet Jake and me just as we finished at the cook car. Whitcomb was the crew boss, the only man mounted on a saddle horse. "Getting an early start!" Whitcomb said to Jake. He pointed to the field, where half a dozen wagons and teams were already lumbering through the scattered grain shocks. Two or three men walked beside each wagon, pitching the bundles up to the stacker, their fork tines catching the gleam of the early-morning sun.

Suddenly I heard Mr. Gunderson hollering. He was standing beside a monstrous, vibrating machine, urgently motioning for me to come over. He thrust a bundle fork into my hands and pushed me toward a wagon that was just trundling up to one side of the conveyor. "Jump up there now and start pitchin'," he ordered.

I scrambled up fast and stabbed my fork into a bundle, then leaned back on the handle to lift the heavy load. "Keep the bundles comin'!" Mr. Gunderson snapped. "Al there is in charge of the grain separator. You got to keep him happy or we'll send you back to help the cook!" I awkwardly thumped the first bundle on the conveyor and glanced up to see Al atop his clamoring machine, watching me closely. I stabbed my fork into the next bundle thinking how slow and clumsy I was.

"Do it like this," the wagon driver instructed, keeping his back straight as he bent his knees to lift his bundles. I tried my best to heft them the way he showed me. The oat bundles were heavy and my back was already complaining, but I reminded myself that any job was better than peeling potatoes for the cook.

The bundle wagons lumbered in steadily, leaving no time to dawdle. Al Swenson kept a sharp eye on us. He wanted the bundles fed right, not too fast and not too slow. Even his dog, Buddy, panting in the shade under the separator, seemed to have one eye trained on the spike pitchers.

In what seemed like no time Al shouted for me to

run to the cook car for everybody's lunch. It was already nine o'clock, time for sandwiches and cake. I ran as fast as I could in case Mr. Gunderson was watching. Buddy bounded right beside me.

"Might as well take enough for McGraith, too," the cook grunted. "He's working the steam engine." He filled steaming mugs with strong coffee for the men and a tall glass with lemonade for me. I grabbed a sandwich off the plate and took a bite, breaking a chunk off for Buddy, too.

The cook thumped the coffee mugs into a large, round pan. "You're hungry," he remarked, sounding pleased. He slapped two more sandwiches onto the stack before waving me on my way. I *was* hungry. I had wolfed down the extra sandwiches by the time I got back to the separator.

Hearing a shout, I glanced up to see Al waving his fists and hollering at Mr. McGraith on the steam engine. His words couldn't be heard above the slapping belts and crunch and clatter of the machine.

"We're losing power!" Al exploded as I held up the plates of sandwiches and cake to him. "Run over and tell that fool to fire up his boiler!" He snatched some food and I ran to the steam engine.

Mr. McGraith looked up from his gauges long enough to help himself to the last three sandwiches.

"Al says he needs more power," I told him, breathing hard.

Mr. McGraith looked at me sternly. "That's all Al ever says," he replied. Then he winked. "I say *he's* feeding the bundles too fast, but don't bother to tell him I said so."

I grinned.

"Boy! Quit your daydreaming and get back to work!" Mr. Gunderson thundered at me, rumbling past in an empty grain wagon. I scrambled as fast as I could to the cook car, returning plates, before I scurried back to grab my pitchfork.

Just before dinner at noon, Jake drove Babe and Black up to the separator with a load of bundles. He jumped down and snatched my fork, setting it against the wagon. "Run get yourself a drink of water while I start this load," he ordered. Jake seemed to know my muscles were aching.

The run felt good. Buddy frolicked along beside me, grinning his doggy grin. The warm sun and the high blue sky felt friendly, as if they'd muscled out the wind for a change. I liked the busy clatter of the separator and the slap-flap of the rotating belts. It made me feel that I was part of something big.

The noon meal was a huge spread of roast beef and potatoes and gravy, pickled beets and creamed peas, fresh bread and apple pie. It was my job to deliver plates to Al and Mr. McGraith before I ran back to get my own food. I had just opened my mouth for the first bite when Mr. Gunderson caught my eye. "You there," he boomed, "come with me! We need to fill the feed bags so these horses can eat. Then you'll have time for your dinner." I glanced longingly at my plate and set it down.

"Scoop this much into each bag," he told me, dipping the first bag in the oat pile and showing me how much he'd put in, "and slip the strap over their ears like so." He watched me slide a feed bag over the nose of one of the horses before he grunted, as if he might be just a little bit satisfied. Then he left me there to feed the others while he hurried to catch up with one of the bundle haulers. I measured the bags carefully, but I didn't dawdle. Mr. Gunderson was probably watching from somewhere.

After dinner everyone seemed to tear into his work with renewed energy. I thought we must be just like the horses and steam engine, needing plenty of fuel and water to keep going. But no matter how hard I tried I couldn't lift the bundles fast enough, and they were so heavy they always landed on the conveyor with an awkward thump. Sometimes I caught the wagon driver eyeing me as he pitched his bundles smooth and even, but I just gritted my teeth and tried to work harder, ignoring the ache in my arms and back.

As the afternoon passed, the straw pile grew higher and higher and the sun beat down on us in a white heat. Sweat dripped into my eyes. The pain in my shoulders and arms was only a dull throb now, and I imagined my back getting stronger with every lift. I swiped at my brow when I had to, and kept on pitching.

"John Whitcomb is a smart operator, a good man to work for," Mr. McGraith confided to me late in the afternoon when I climbed up between wagons to bring his four o'clock lunch. "You and your daddy don't need to worry about this crew being slackers. That's the trick to keep from having your luck turn against you—every man has to stay sharp."

I wasn't sure what he meant about luck turning against us, unless he was meaning the weather. But men staying sharp couldn't change the whims of the weather, anybody knew that. I didn't correct him about Mr. Gunderson not being my daddy either. I just grinned like I'd seen Jake do and said what I'd heard him say: "Yep, they're a fine crew!"

All through the afternoon, the wagons rumbled steadily in from the field. Then at supper time one of the horses turned up lame. I heard Mr. Gunderson and John Whitcomb talking it over and Mr. Gunderson mentioning his young team at home. "Well, let's put the boy to driving a wagon then," Whitcomb suggested. "Harley here can rest his lame horse and take over spike pitching, and the boy can bring your team out in the morning. He could ride along with someone in the field now and learn the ropes."

I tried not to let the eagerness show on my face as I watched Mr. Gunderson think it over. "We *do* need a stronger man pitching bundles," he said. Then to me, "You go out in the field and find Jake. Tell him to show you how to handle a team with a load of bundles."

I threw down my fork without waiting to hear more. Even though I suspected I'd been dismissed because I was pitching too slow, it was such a relief to be free of it, I felt glad. My back and arms tingled as I ran, and I knew they were even happier than me that our spike pitching hitch was done.

I told Jake Mr. Gunderson's plan, and he moved over and handed me the reins. In no time I was driving the team around the field while Jake did the stacking in the back of the wagon. We worked together until Jake said it was time to pitch off our load and go home to do the milking. "You had enough of this for one day?" he asked me.

I had to grin at him in spite of how tired and stiff I felt.

"You're doing a good job of driving," he added as I turned the team to head for home. I wished Mr. Gunderson was there to hear his words. But even so, hearing them myself gave me the fire I needed to face the milking when my muscles were telling me to crawl under a bundle stack and drift off to sleep.

The Wind Plays Its Hand

When Mrs. Gunderson called me, I could barely believe it was morning. I moaned and rolled over. My whole body ached.

Mr. Gunderson was currying the horses and the cows were already stepping through the door when I got to the barn. The eastern sky was just blushing pink across the horizon, it was that early. I grabbed the feed bucket and scattered oats into the mangers, feeling pain flash through my muscles with every move.

"If we hurry we can eat with the crew at the cook car," Jake told me. His words made me forget about my aches. I couldn't wait to be back working with the crew.

I was milking Rosie as fast as I could when I heard Mr. Gunderson's step on the hard dirt of the barn floor. He stopped, staring around at the rows of cows.

I'd forgotten the little white paper names I'd nailed over each manger.

"What's going on here?" he demanded, scowling. "Looks like you had plenty of leisure time while I was gone." His voice was sharp with sarcasm. He turned and glared hard at me and I felt hot shame burn up my neck. "I want those things taken down," he said. "You come out here to work! The sooner you get that through your thick skull, the better off you'll be. I can't help it they treat you like babies at that orphanage. We don't have time—*you* better not have time—to be doing such nonsense. Do I make myself clear?"

I nodded, swallowing hard.

"Soon as you're done milkin'. But do it fast—ain't nobody going to stand around waitin' for you, you understand me?"

"Yes, sir." I nodded harder.

Mr. Gunderson turned and stomped out.

I didn't know how I'd grab the name tags down without taking time from turning the separator crank, but I was determined I'd do it somehow. I milked so fast and hard that Rosie lifted a leg and landed a kick that knocked me clean off the stool.

I was almost done with Bess when Jake came past on his way to the separator room. He set his pail inside the door and came back to Elsie, the first cow. He did something quickly and went on to the next cow. I stretched my neck around and saw that he was pulling off the name tags. My heart sank, fearing he was mad at me, too. What would I do if he told me to forget about driving the team, ever?

I saw his boots out of the corner of my eye as he came up even with me. My heart was hammering as he stopped and leaned an arm on Bessie's rump, waiting for me to pause in my frantic milking and look up at him. To my relief his eyes were kindly. "Harvest is a tough time for everybody," he said quietly. "Delton says more than he means sometimes."

I let out a sigh of relief. "It was a dumb thing to do," I muttered, wanting Jake to know I was sorry for causing such trouble.

Jake cocked his head to one side, looking thoughtful. Then he shook his head. "Taking the tags down don't make the naming a bad idea—it don't make it wrong just cause somebody else don't like it." He opened his hand and showed me the papers fitted squarely, one on top of the other, in his palm. "You want to keep 'em?"

"No," I said, surprised he'd even ask.

"All right. I'll put 'em in my stove, then. Make nice kindling the first fire this fall." He smiled, and I dared smile back.

"Thank you, Jake," I said.

He gave me a wink and strode unhurried back to the separator room. As though his time was his own, I thought. As though his brother had no say in that, no matter if it was harvest.

When we got done milking, Mr. Gunderson had the wagons all ready. He led the way to the threshing field with Joe and Jen, and I drove Babe and Black. The Missus followed with Pet and Pal while Jake took up the rear with Buster and Bonnie. The excitement of driving a team again shoved the name tags from my mind.

Driving the bundle wagon was a pleasure—the field pitchers joked and laughed as they walked along either side of my wagon, pitching the bundles up to the man who stacked them in place. As the day warmed, I felt my confidence growing. "You're doin' a good job, sonny," the stacker said with a grin when he heard me whistling on our second trip out to the field. "Makes a fella feel good, don't it?"

I grinned back at him.

"Maybe we'll get this field off without a hitch," he said. Then he glanced up at the sky as if he wondered if he'd spoken too soon. It made me quit my whistling and tend to business. Every man on the crew did have to be sharp, I'd learned that much. No use taking chances.

Still, everything went smoothly that second day, and by the third we had finished the oats and were threshing wheat like a great oiled machine. Jake had taken over hauling the grain to the bins, and Mr. Gunderson now drove the water wagon. Most times he was pumping water from his tank into the steam engine's boiler when I drove up with my bundles. I sat up as straight and tall as I could, with a firm grip on the reins, so he would have no cause to fault my driving.

Late in the morning the wind picked up, a welcome breeze that whisked away the sun's heat and dried the prickly sweat on my neck and forehead. It was a fidgety wind, puffing up little clusters of chaff and straw and teasing them off, first one way and then another. The men never let up their pace, never seemed to notice much whether it was windy or scorching hot. They went about their business as if time was the only thing that mattered—getting as much done as quick as they could while everything was running the way it ought to.

Then, close to noon, just as I was driving my wagon in from the field, I spotted the first blaze.

Fire!

My mouth dried out so sudden that I couldn't seem to pry my tongue loose to shout. I knew right away what must have happened—the wind had whiffed a spark from the steam engine smokestack to the growing straw pile.

The straw hauler was busily unloading his wagon next to the firebox. He hadn't seen the flames. No one had.

"Fire!" I rasped hoarsely; my lungs couldn't get enough air to shout. I gave Babe and Black an excited slap with the reins that made them bolt against the traces.

"*Fire!*" I yelled louder, waving my hat to get somebody's attention. Mr. Gunderson looked up from pumping water into the boiler and stared hard in my direction.

"*FIRE!*" I hollered, near splitting my voice box. The sound couldn't reach him. I gestured frantically toward the straw pile before a jolt of the wagon sent me sprawling to my knees.

Finally Mr. Gunderson caught sight of the flames. He scrambled to the wagon seat and slapped the reins, sending his team bolting past the steam engine. I saw him holler something to the bundle haulers as he went by. Mr. McGraith pumped three sharp blasts on the steam whistle. I made my trembling hands whoa Babe and Black, unable to think what I should do next.

The wind chose that moment to kick up its heels. Flames leaped up, shooting sprays of bright orange and red everywhere. My heart hammered louder than the clattering separator as I stared at those licking flames. By now everyone had heard the steam whistle, and wagons from all over the field came jolting in, picking up men who were running to help.

"Leave your horses here, boy!" somebody yelled as he ran by. His words woke me up. I flung the reins over the crosstree, jumped down, and ran through the stubble.

"Move the wagon! Get my grain out of here!" Mr. Gunderson ordered the straw hauler. "You, boy, go unhitch a team so we can move the separator!"

I turned uncertainly back to Babe and Black. My throat was dry as dust. Could I unhitch a team by myself?

Mr. Gunderson swore loudly. "Dammit, boy! Use *this* team here! They're closer!"

I spun around in confusion and stumbled off in the direction he pointed. The flames crackled through the straw pile, bounding so high that Mr. Gunderson whipped his team to get the water tank to safety. The fire snarled and spat just like in my dreams; the acrid smell stung my nostrils and nipped my eyes. I longed to shut it all out—if only I could run the other way and never look back!

But even though my heart was thumping like to burst, my legs somehow kept me running forward. One of the men ran past, driving a team in front of him. "Over here, boy!" Mr. Gunderson barked. "Grab that doubletree!"

I scrabbled to drag it into place as the men backed the horses, forcing my shaking hands to hook up the tree while Al ran to the front and rigged the tongue to the harness.

"Look out! Get out of the way!" Al bellowed at me. Just in time, I staggered to the side as Mr. Gunderson hawed the horses away.

I gulped in a shuddering breath, willing my heart to stop beating itself to death. Slow down, I thought, trying to breathe easy, but I couldn't get enough air.

"It's heading for the field!" someone shouted. The flames were leaping from the straw pile now, streaking in every direction as the wind chased them one way and then another. Men ran with shovels to whack at the slithering fingers of flame; others grabbed burlap bags from a stack on the water wagon and soaked them in what little water remained in the tank before running to beat at the blaze.

I stared at the hissing snakes of fire, and my legs turned to stumps, too heavy to move. It seemed to come from everywhere—raging all around me—driven by the all-powerful prairie wind. How could the men ever hope to stop it?

A furious roar made me whirl in terror. The fire had devoured the first shock of grain. I ran—blindly stumbling through the rough stubble. Blistering heat seared my back, and I thought for a moment the fire was reaching out to grab me, too, when—*smack!* I collided with something solid.

"Where you going? What you doing?" Mr. Gunderson's bellow sent me reeling backward.

He grasped my arms and spun me around, shoving me roughly back toward the field. "Help 'em! Everybody's got to help!" he hollered. I scrambled forward, unable to see anything but flames and smoke. Someone thrust a wet sack in my hands and I found myself on the line of defense. The men battered the flames with their wet bags and stomped with their boots, and I did the same. I couldn't see through the sweat and tears, and the sound in my ears was like the din of a freight engine. I beat with my sack dumbly, not even knowing whether I struck at flames or was only beating the dirt. I didn't care. I was too confused, too scared, too shamed by my running to do anything but beat and stomp and let the wind and fire do whatever they would to me.

"Get back! Get back!" It was Jake's voice and Jake's arm pulling me around as we turned to fight the flames coming at us from a new direction.

We fought for what seemed like hours. Until, on some new whim, the wind shifted, blowing the flames around the way they had come. Smaller flares tried to lick forward, but with the wind on our side we were finally able to pummel them back into their own blackened circle.

Suddenly I heard cheering around me and, looking up, I realized the fire was out.

We'd done it!

The men laughed and jostled one another as they all gathered beside the water wagon. We'd saved the separator and the steam engine and all but about twenty acres of the field. Somebody slapped me on the back.

"Thank God the wind switched," someone said.

"Good thing you spotted the fire, boy," Al declared, grinning. Jake, too, clapped a hand on my shoulder as if Al's words made him proud. My heart thumped hard, glad for their words, but not feeling deserving. My parched throat wouldn't have let me speak even if I'd known what to say.

Mr. Gunderson was the only one who didn't join in the merriment. His eyes burned like coals and his face was dark and thunderous. "Twenty acres!" he spat.

Suddenly it was so quiet that all I could hear was the sound of feet shuffling in the crisp, dry stubble.

"Could have lost a lot more than twenty acres if the wind hadn't switched," Mr. McGraith spoke up.

Mr. Gunderson seemed not to hear. "I knew I should have found one more water wagon," he muttered as if he were talking to himself. "And one more man. Can't run a threshin' outfit without enough strong men."

I felt a chill cut through me—I knew what Mr. Gunderson was thinking.

John Whitcomb glanced around the circle of threshers. His face was stern when his eyes settled on Mr. Gunderson. "It was the wind," he said. "Wind that started it, wind that sent it back again. We ought to be grateful no more damage was done. Everyone pitched in and did a fine job here today. Now let's see if we can hook things back up and get the steam rolling again. Andy, how soon you going to be ready with dinner?"

There was more good-natured jostling as the men

started back to their jobs. Several followed Mr. McGraith to help reposition the steam engine and hook up the belts.

I wanted to walk off with the others, but I couldn't do it. My stomach pitched crazily, expecting any minute Mr. Gunderson would holler again. Jake still stood beside him, looking as though he was about to say something, but the words must have stuck in his throat. He gave his brother one long, steady look before he turned and strode after the others.

That left Mr. Gunderson alone, scowling into the ashes. I knew he wasn't wasting time being mad at the wind. For sure he wasn't grateful to God for sending it back on its heels, either. Mr. Gunderson respected power when he saw it. It was weakness made him mad. There was only one person had earned his fury.

That person was me. The only one who'd turned and run.

＊ ＊ ＊

That night a raging fire burned through my dreams. I screamed and screamed for someone to notice, but no sound came out. I tried to run for water, but my legs wouldn't move any faster than those of a mule sucked down in the mud. Fire crackled and roared around me. The heat blistered my cheeks.

I woke up as I threw myself forward, flinging my arms over my scorching face.

"FIRE!" The shout from my parched throat echoed in my ears and I found I was gasping for air, at the same time listening with every muscle tensed for fear I'd wakened the Gundersons.

What if Mr. Gunderson were to find out about my dreams? What would he say if he knew a dream could scare me this bad, could wake me up screaming and sweating and fighting to breathe? What if he knew I'd feared this day—and dreamed of it—as long as I could remember?

The house was silent. Slowly I sank back down on the goose-feather pillow. I kept my eyes open as long as I could, hoping the fires in my head would burn out before my tired mind pulled me back to sleep.

Schoolyard Conspiracy

After the threshing crew had moved on, we stayed busy at the Gundersons', hauling the grain to town and doing the fall chores. Then, true to his word, the first Monday morning in October, Mr. Gunderson sent me off across the field to get my education.

Hawkeye School was a white clapboard building set on a little hill a mile away from the Gundersons' farm. Its rows of tall windows frowned down side by side like watchful soldiers, while the peaked bell tower pointed like an arrow at the sky. Coarse prairie grass formed a ragged playground around the school.

I was surprised to see girls pivoting lazily back and forth on the swings. Others were shrieking, chasing one another through the grass. There had been no girls at the orphanage. The boys looked up from their game of Pum-pum-pull-away and eyed me warily. I kept my distance, eyeing them back. One of the bigger boys turned and muttered something to his friend, and they both laughed.

I stood my ground.

The bigger one sobered, looking me over. "You the orphan just come to the Gundersons'?" he asked. There was something about the way he said *orphan* and the way they all looked me over, letting him speak for them, that made me think I was maybe the first of my kind they'd ever seen.

"Yeah," I said.

"You're late," he stated sullenly. "School started two weeks ago."

I didn't know what it mattered to him. Or to any of them. Mr. Gunderson had written a note addressed to the schoolmaster, Mr. Wolverton, explaining that I'd been helping with harvest. But I could see the older boys chalked up my absence as a sign of ignorance. A high-tailed skunk would have been regarded with less suspicion if he'd showed up at Hawkeye School.

Just at that moment someone pulled the rope and the bell in the tower clanged loudly. I realized it was these deep, clear tones I'd heard faintly across the fields at the Gundersons', mornings when I came up from milking. We lined up at the bottom of the steps, the girls eagerly finding a place in the front, the boys jostling to the end of the line. I held back and took my place behind them all.

From the top of the steps Mr. Wolverton studied us soberly, tapping a blackboard pointer on the palm of his hand. He was a man of slight build, with coal black hair that shone as if he'd greased it before he combed it straight back. His ebony topcoat with its pointed lapels made me think of shovel blades.

"Good morning. Please file in," he commanded in a flat voice.

The upper-grade classroom was flanked with tall windows and black chalkboards. The desks were bolted to the floor in five straight rows that reminded me of Mr. Wolverton's straight-back hair and the razor lines of his coat. I felt everyone's eyes on me as I shambled to the front of the room and handed the schoolmaster the note Mr. Gunderson had sent with me. He read it quickly and glanced at the back of the room. "Mike," he said in the same somber tone, "give this new boy your desk and move your things to the back table with Pete."

One of the girls giggled as I strode to my assigned seat. I kept my eyes straight in front of me, feeling my ears and neck burn red in embarrassment. Mike, one of the boys who'd laughed at me on the playground, gave me a wary glance as he gathered his things and strode to the back table. His friend, Pete, was already seated there, and they grinned at each other, clearly pleased to be sitting together.

We all stood and recited the Pledge of Allegiance, and as Mr. Wolverton took roll and began calling out the day's assignments, everyone seemed to lose interest in me. I felt out of place, alone, and my thoughts drifted back to Acorn; if my brother were here he'd have already made himself some friends, I was sure of it. Everyone liked Acorn. Then with a stab of guilt I thought of the promise I'd made him—and that I hadn't written him, even to say I still remembered what I'd promised.

I opened my arithmetic book and found the page, but Acorn's face was there, a trick of my mind, sketched in darker lines than the numbers on the page. I blinked and his image faded, but the look in his eyes stayed etched in my mind. How was my brother feeling now? Surely things had gotten better—Acorn had a lot of friends at the orphanage.

Someone behind me whispered something, and there was a flash of pink from across the aisle. It bought me back to Hawkeye School. I licked my lips and found my place on the page. Now and then I heard a whisper and I thought I heard the word *orphan*, but I didn't look around.

I was just finishing my sums when I became aware of a tap-tapping from close by. Darting a glance across the aisle, I found a pair of bright green eyes laughing at me. It was a girl about my age, bouncing her pencil on the rim of the inkwell of her desk. I skimmed my eyes away fast, but not before I glimpsed her gleaming black boot merrily tapping the floor and the curve of a white stocking disappearing under the pink flounce of her skirt. I felt another hot red blush creeping up the back of my neck.

There was a snort from behind me. I shot a quick look at the teacher, but his back was turned to us as he explained an assignment to the sixth graders. Turning around, I spotted Pete and Mike both smirking at me, then glancing meaningfully toward the girl's bowed yellow head. They were teasing me for blushing just because of a girl's smile. I shrugged, trying to act as if I didn't care. But I couldn't stop my ears from burning when I caught the sound of another stifled laugh.

There seemed to be new rules here at Hawkeye School. I had a lot to learn, and not just things written in books. I could see I'd better keep my eyes wide open.

* * *

"Bring your lunch around back of the school. We got to talk," Pete muttered to me as he passed by my desk for noon recess.

My heart gave a little lurch of anticipation. I'd been in school for over a week and this was the first time anyone had invited me to eat with them. Pete was the last person I'd expected to do it, although he had grudgingly let me join in the older boys' games when he saw I wouldn't try to run things. I clapped down the lid on the syrup can that held my lunch and followed Pete and Mike outside.

Helen glanced up and winked from her seat next to mine. She was always laughing and tossing her yellow curls. I couldn't decide if she was making fun of me or it was just her way of seeing what I was made of.

Pete and Mike slipped quickly down the steps. I hurried behind them. They went around to the back of the schoolhouse and sat cross-legged in the grass. We all opened our lunch pails.

"It true you been in an orphanage all these years?" Pete asked me, taking a bite out of a sandwich.

"Yeah, it's true," I admitted.

"Good," Pete said. "That way we figure you ain't no sissy."

His face was open and friendly. I grinned a little. "No, I don't figure I'm a sissy," I said.

Pete and Mike smirked at each other. "Good! We thought you might like to get in on a little fun."

I pulled out my sandwich and took a bite, waiting.

"There's a kid, you see. Sixth grader. Thinks he's the cat's meow, know what I mean?"

I nodded slowly, watching his face for any sign of him smirking at Mike again. I didn't want the two of them making fun of me.

"This kid Leroy Johnson. Know him?"

I shook my head.

"I'll show you who he is in a minute. Him and his friends thought it would be funny to put a burr under my saddle. I caught him yesterday after school just as he was leaving, and his friends run off. I asked him what he thought he was doing, and he got real cocky. Said it was none of my business."

I knew Pete and some of the other kids rode to school on horseback and kept their horses in the barn.

"I got a plan," Pete went on. "Mike and me came up with it this morning. I could use your help, if you ain't afraid."

"What's your plan?" I asked guardedly.

"Are you with us? See, we got to know you're with us before we tell what we got in mind."

I hesitated.

"Maybe we figured you wrong," Pete said, glancing at Mike. "See, Mike and me stick together, and we're looking for another guy that understands how sometimes it comes in handy to have a friend."

When he put it that way, I couldn't see I had anything to lose. I wouldn't mind having a friend myself. "Count me in," I said.

Pete and Mike grinned.

"I'm giving you the easy part," Pete began. "Mike and me will go down to the barn as soon as ol' Wolverton lets us out of school this afternoon. You hang back and keep an eye on Leroy Johnson. Just walk slow behind him.

"Leroy lives down the road a ways," Pete continued. "Sometimes he walks, sometimes he rides a horse. When his friends get on the buses, you come up behind him and tell him you want to ask him something."

I wet my lips, concentrating. This didn't sound hard at all.

"Ask him to show you something in the barn. Say you're thinking of bringing your horse to school and you wonder is there room for another. Say you're new here if he wonders why you're asking him."

I nodded quickly. "That all?" I asked.

Pete glanced at Mike. "Just make sure he goes to the barn," Mike put in. "You go with him, maybe ask some more questions to make him think he's really doing a big thing for you."

Pete laughed, a loud horse laugh. "Yeah, a big thing," he repeated, slapping a hand on Mike's shoulder. "He'll like that. Then, once he's there, make sure you get him to come all the way in. He might get scared if he sees Mike and me, and we don't want him runnin' off."

"We'll be out of sight," Mike put in.

"Right," Pete said. "Don't look for us. Keep asking him things so he don't get suspicious. If there's anybody else in the barn, just keep talking to Leroy 'cause we got to wait to make our move till everybody else is gone home."

I thought about it. It seemed as if I'd have to think up a lot of questions. "How long you planning to wait before you show yourselves?" I asked.

"Not long. Not long at all," Pete assured me. Mike nodded fiercely in agreement. "You can take off for home soon as we come out, if you want. That's all there is to it."

It wasn't too much to ask of a pal. I was already thinking up questions I could pump at old Leroy to keep him busy.

"There he is!" Mike grabbed Pete's elbow and pointed as three boys came into view, jostling each other. "He's the one in the middle."

Leroy Johnson spun and chased his friend to tag him. I hadn't caught his name before, but I'd noticed him. He was small for his age, a head shorter than either of his two friends; his skin was white as milk with brown freckles splotched over it, his cheeks fiery red. All his features were so vividly colored, so delicately drawn, it was as if someone had painted them there. But his eyes were what had really caught my attention. They were bright blue, but they had a flash of expression that was like my brother's, shining the way Acorn's eyes shone when he had an escapade to report. Every time I noticed Leroy, I wondered what Acorn would have been like if he were growing up on the open prairie and not shut inside an orphanage.

"He's pretty as a girl," Pete snickered, his eyes meeting mine like two links in a harness strap. "He's too big for his britches. You know just what to do?"

"I can handle it," I assured him, but having seen who Leroy was, I didn't feel as sure as I sounded.

"Come on," Mike muttered, giving Pete an impatient nudge.

The two of them ran off together, and I followed a little slower. They turned at the schoolhouse corner and Pete motioned to me. "Hurry up! We'll let you be on our side!" he hollered. Then they ran on ahead.

I slowed my steps and stopped as I reached the corner. The upper-grade boys were all lining up to play Kick the Can. I held back, just watching. Even though Pete and Mike had invited me, I felt uneasy joining in. As though it wasn't just the game we were teamed up for, but something else.

Ambush

Leroy Johnson knew all the answers when his sixth-grade class went up to the teacher's desk for geography recitation. Leroy Johnson rated a "Very good!" from Mr. Wolverton for his solutions to the word problems in arithmetic.

I watched when he filed back to his desk behind the other sixth graders. The others kept their eyes on their shoes, their shoulders rounded, scrambling to bury their faces in their books when they got to their seats. Leroy carried himself upright, his shoulders squared, his button blue eyes alert as a rabbit watching for hawks. His eyes met mine just as he reached his desk. He didn't blink but waited until I bent my head forward to open my book. Then he turned and slid into his seat.

I stole a look at the back table. Mike was working sums. Pete met my glance, a little frown flitting off his face as our eyes held. He shrugged his shoulders slightly, his face as blank as if he'd wiped it clean with an eraser.

I turned back to my book. Every time I tried to think of another question for Leroy, I thought instead of another question for Pete. What did he mean about not making his move until everyone was gone home?

"You may close your books," Mr. Wolverton announced, as he did every day at three o'clock. "Check the blackboard for your assignments and take your unfinished work home to complete over the weekend. Don't be coming back Monday morning without your work done!"

I turned around to Pete and Mike, but all I saw were their broad backs disappearing through the door. Helen caught my eye. "Hey!" she said.

I grabbed my books and stumbled past the cloakroom and down the steps. I waited at the bottom for Leroy, hoping he'd come out before Helen did. My heart sank when I saw her slip out the door, giggling and whispering to Mollie, the other girl in the eighth-grade class. Mollie had plain brown hair that she wore in two fat braids. She never giggled. The only time I'd heard her speak was at recitation. And then she'd gotten every answer right.

I dodged behind the wall that formed the edge of the steps, willing the girls to go on by. Helen's voice drifted over my head as she and Mollie strolled toward the end of the playground where the bus wagons were parked. Finally, I dared peek out again. Leroy's bright red shirt bobbed up and down as he marched ramrod straight with two of his friends just a few feet behind Helen and Mollie.

I ambled after them, starting to sweat. What if Leroy escaped and Helen got me cornered with some silly question? What if Leroy's friends hung around, or Leroy got suspicious and started yelling? Pete's plan was nowhere near as simple as he made it sound.

Leroy and his friends stopped to talk while the girls boarded their buses. I scuffed at a rock with the toe of my boot, waiting. Some younger boys hurried by, eyeing me as they passed. I swung around to stare back up at the school, as if I were watching for someone. The next time I looked, I saw Leroy's red shirt moving through the tall grass to the west. He was alone.

I trotted to catch up.

"Hey," I greeted him, friendly-like, falling in step.

He looked up at me coolly, slowing and glancing back toward his pals. I placed myself squarely between him and the buses.

"You know anything about where a fella could keep a horse if he rode one to school?" I asked. My voice came out unnaturally loud.

He eyed me up and down, taking in my cap, overalls, and boots in one disdainful vertical squint. "The barn," he declared, turning on his heel and walking away.

"Which one?" I persisted stupidly, hopping awkwardly through the grass. He was small, but he was quick as a rabbit.

Leroy kept on walking, glancing suspiciously at me and crooking his thumb contemptuously to the other side of the playground, where the only barn for nearly a mile was clearly in view.

"Do you think . . . do you think there's room in it for one more horse?" I puffed.

"How am I supposed to know?" He stopped dead in his tracks to scowl at me, throwing his arms out in pure exasperation at my doltish ignorance.

His expression made me think of Acorn again. "I . . . I thought you might," I said, knowing how lame the words sounded. "Someone said you might know."

His eyes were now a brittle blue, like chips of crushed glass. A shadow clouded them as we faced each other, as if he were calculating reasons why I might want to trick him.

Finally, he sighed and said, "Come on. I'll show you." He turned on his heel and strode purposefully toward the barn.

Relief opened in me like a floodgate. I hadn't let Pete and Mike down. I'd for sure proved I was a real pal.

* * *

The inside of the barn was as dark as a cave except for bright horizontal stripes where the sunlight spilled in through the cracks. My eyes, so full of light from the outside, shut down like a snuffed-out wick.

"I guess we're here. In the barn," I announced loudly. I sounded like a nitwit, but I didn't want Pete and Mike caught by surprise.

Leroy halted suddenly in the darkness and I bumped into him. "Well, there's only one horse here now," he said in an I-told-you-so tone. "He's got the box stall. Looks like you'd have room to bring a whole herd."

"I suppose," I answered, stepping around Leroy and backing deeper into the barn to draw him in.

Just then two shadowy forms pushed past me. My heart sprang right up my throat.

"What're you doing?" Leroy bellowed. Instantly there was a sharp slap of a hand on his mouth and then a howl from Pete.

"Little brat bit me!" Pete screeched.

My eyes were adjusting to the dim light. I could see both Pete and Mike clamp a hold on Leroy's struggling figure.

"Lemme go! Lemme go!" Leroy hollered.

A fist smacked into soft flesh with a sickening *thwump!*

"Leave me alone! Get away from me!" Leroy choked out, squirming and kicking at them as they yanked his arms behind his back and tied his wrists.

I backed away into the dusty shadows, suddenly sorry I'd tricked Leroy into coming here.

"Grab ahold of his legs!" I heard Pete order, his breath rasping.

"I'm tryin'!" Mike snapped.

Leroy started bellowing for help.

"Get somethin' to stuff in his mouth!" Pete thundered angrily. There was the dull thud of a fist again.

Leroy's hollers diminished to bleats as Mike apparently followed Pete's orders. Then they half rolled him over in the straw. "Let's tie his feet," Pete commanded, breathing hard.

I watched them truss Leroy's wrists and ankles together, feeling sicker by the minute. I'd really gotten Leroy in a mess.

"You listen good, little Leroy Johnson," I heard

Pete snarl. "We're gonna show you what can happen to them that fools with others' horses. Teach you a lesson so's you won't forget another time."

My heart was hammering. I'd meant to run as soon as I had the chance, but I was frozen there in the shadows. Frozen with guilt. Frozen with fear.

"This here horse you fooled with is a mean one," Pete went on. "He's a kicker. Real mean kicker. Feels somethin' behind him he don't know what it is, he gives it a good hard kick, quick as lightning."

Leroy's body jerked in the straw. As if he thought he could break those ropes loose with one mighty twist. Mike gave a hollow, scoffing laugh.

"Here, loop this over the rafter," Pete ordered, handing Mike a coiled rope.

I saw the rope snake up into the air. Pete looped one end around Leroy's chest and drew it tight.

"We're gonna swing you high now," Pete said stepping close to Leroy, "Right in front of the stall gate where my ol' horse is waitin'."

Leroy jerked his body in protest, but Mike pulled hard on the far end of the rope, hoisting him up.

There was a flurry of thumps as the horse stomped the hard-packed dirt of the stall floor as though he was uneasy with all the commotion. Then Pete swung the gate open and Leroy gave out a muffled yowl.

"Let 'im down a little," Pete commanded, stepping back at right angles to the horse's hooves and grabbing up a willow switch that was leaning against the stall rail.

I saw the light color on the tip of the switch where someone had whittled a sharp point. And I saw the flex of Pete's fingers as he gripped it. His free hand shot up, a signal to Mike to hold steady. Leroy's body dangled about knee high to Pete, just the right height for a calculated kick. The horse was prancing now, his hooves clumping against either side of the stall as he shuffled nervously one way and then the other.

"Steady," Pete cautioned. Whether he spoke to the horse or Mike or both, I couldn't be sure. Cold beads of sweat popped out on my forehead. I wanted to run in and cut Leroy down, but I knew I couldn't fight both Pete and Mike.

Suddenly Pete jabbed the stick hard into the horse's hind leg. At the same time Mike heaved back with a mighty grunt, whipping Leroy's slack body up—sending him twirling like a top just as horse hooves exploded.

The next instant Pete sprang to swing the stall gate shut. As he rammed the bolt into place, there was a splintering crash of hooves against wood.

Leroy dangled limp as a rag. I held my breath,

scared he'd fainted. Then a terrible thought—what if they'd somehow killed him?

Pete grabbed the rope and pulled Leroy toward him. "You don't breathe a word to anyone about this. You hear me?" He warned in a low growl.

To my relief, Leroy's head dipped up and down frantically.

"You or your friends gonna give me any more trouble?"

Leroy's head shook in a frenzy.

"Don't forget!" Pete spat before he signaled Mike to let Leroy loose.

I didn't stay to see more. I backed up as quietly as I could and staggered out the door. Stumbling through the grass toward the road, I tried to hurry my legs, but it took a while before they seemed to want to hold me upright. I was sick. Sick at what I'd seen, sick at what I'd done.

Suddenly I heard the sound of a door slamming, and I jumped as if I'd heard a shot. Behind the school a figure was striding down from the outhouse. I could see Mr. Wolverton's topcoat flapping and his elbows cutting sharp angles in the air as he marched toward the barn. His hand flew up and he hollered something as he caught sight of me.

Panic nearly choked me. Without even thinking

what would happen next, I wheeled around and ran, lunging blindly down the trail, then across the field toward the Gundersons' farm. I didn't look back, just kept on running until the sounds of my own breath drowned out Mr. Wolverton's shouts.

I was in real trouble now. I knew it for sure.

Swift Judgment

While I was doing chores after school and helping Jake and Mr. Gunderson with the milking, all I could think was, when would Mr. Wolverton appear? Jake glanced at me a couple of times as if he could tell something was wrong, but I just tried to make myself look busier. When the Missus asked at supper if I felt unwell, I told the truth, that my stomach ached so bad I couldn't eat, and she sent me off to bed.

Being in my room didn't help. It took a long time to fall asleep. When I did, the fires raged through my dreams, and as I cried for help I saw Mr. Wolverton chasing after me with a flaming blackboard pointer.

It was a relief to open my eyes and see sunlight streaming in the window. I shuffled down to breakfast, glad I had survived the night but knowing I was getting closer to Mr. Wolverton's wrath with every passing minute.

"You're tired this morning." Mrs. Gunderson observed. "Good thing it's Saturday."

For a second I felt relief—at least I didn't have to go to school. But then I felt the dread again. I'd be worn to a frazzle from worry by Monday. I shoveled in a spoonful of oatmeal and did my best to swallow it even when it stuck in my throat. Washing it down with coffee, I made myself take another slurp. I couldn't afford to be late for milking and have Mr. Gunderson asking questions.

That cool fall morning the Missus was set to butcher chickens. She had customers in town for twenty of her old laying hens. After we'd finished milking, I followed Jake as he slipped quietly into the closed henhouse. He carried a long crook fashioned from smooth wire to grasp the legs of the sleepy chickens. As he pulled each hen to him, he grabbed her feet in his strong hands and let her dangle upside down. He handed the first two to me before snagging two more. My stomach started pitching dangerously as I followed Jake outside, holding the wide-eyed chickens at arm's length and swallowing hard, fighting desperately not to lose my breakfast.

Jake stopped at the chopping block. The first

whack of the axe made me jump so I almost dropped the hens. I hung on, though, shutting my eyes tight, willing away the sight I'd glimpsed of blood splattering everywhere and the glassy-eyed head rolling away. I heard Jake grunt something and felt him nudge me to hand over a bird. When I opened my eyes, the headless bodies of the first hens were scuttling around in a crazy dance in the farmyard dust. I gasped a quick breath before I clamped my mouth tight shut, trying not to remember the feel of the scaly claws in my hands. My stomach rolled again and I swallowed hard, focusing my eyes on the first chicken, who lay still at last, with the wind teasing her feathers.

"Let's go for more," Jake said, brushing past me on his way back to the henhouse. I followed him, grateful for the cool breeze, fighting dizziness that made my knees wobbly. The chickens were clucking impatiently on their roosts, eager to be let out for breakfast. Still, when Jake got ahold of their feet they never struggled or let out a peep. I wondered if they knew about the chopping block or if they thought the upside-down ride was a treat, a load off their scraggly-toed feet. I wondered if their last moments were happy ones. Then, before I could stop myself, I thought about Mr. Wolverton again, and I wondered if the chickens and I had more in common today than I wanted to imagine.

Mr. and Mrs. Gunderson lugged two heavy boilers out to the yard. The Missus dipped each headless bird into the boiler of steaming water, then she plunged it, dripping, into the boiler of cold water and handed each of us one to pluck.

The touch of the scaly, lifeless claws and the feel of the warmish feathers made my stomach roll again, but I was determined to ignore my pitching insides and work as hard as anyone. Maybe if the Gundersons found out what I'd done at school they'd remember how hard I'd worked today and believe I hadn't meant Leroy any harm. I paid close attention when Jake showed me how to strip the large feathers off quickly in fat handfuls, first the tail and wings, and then the body, front and back. The last was the hardest part, as each wet pinfeather had to be pinched out.

The Missus busied herself, between chickens, hustling back and forth from the kitchen with more kettles of steaming water. She inspected each of my finished birds carefully, making a little *tsk* sound with her tongue, then handed me another dripping chicken before she set about gleaning every remaining pinfeather from my finished bird. I was glad when she found a few stray feathers on Mr. Gunderson's and Jake's chickens, too.

When we had plucked all of them, we scrabbled their naked, limp bodies in our arms and carried them inside, dropping them in a helter-skelter pile on the counter by the stove. Mr. Gunderson and Jake carried the table in and Mrs. Gunderson handed me a warm, soapy rag to wash it down. Then Jake removed two of the flat, round lids from the top of the coal stove and solemnly lifted each chicken, rotating it over the flame, singeing the hairs from their pasty white bodies. The smell stung my nostrils worse than the mustard plaster a nurse had put on my chest once when I was sick in the infirmary.

Between the heat of the kitchen and the smells, my stomach went into full revolt. The Missus started to ask about lunch, but I couldn't wait around to hear. I tore out the door.

Just as I reached the clothesline, I saw a buggy turn into the yard. I didn't know who was driving the team, but I knew who was sitting straight as a rail beside him, his ebony coat and hat gleaming sharp as blackened coals. Clapping a hand over my mouth, I sprinted for the outhouse.

I was sick all right. Sick and sorry and doomed. Puking my insides out was a dreadful thing, as though a sharp stick was raking my body clean, pushing everything up and out. But I knew the pain and chills and shivering tears were nothing compared to what was waiting for me at the house.

✳ ✳ ✳

I stayed in the dark privy long after my stomach had settled down and I could breathe almost normally again. I leaned my forehead on my arms on the bench. I'd never been so sick. It was no great place to be if your nose was working, but still I stayed there as long as I dared, hoping everyone would forget about me and leave.

"*Boy!*" I heard Mr. Gunderson shout from the house. I stood up slowly, feeling my stomach teeter with the movement, and made myself push open the door. The bright sunlight nearly blinded me, but I could see Mr. Gunderson standing on the porch, talking to the schoolmaster and the other man. Taking a deep breath, I stumbled out the door, losing my hold so it slapped shut behind me. They all turned and stared.

"Git over here, boy! Now!" Mr. Gunderson barked.

I ran my tongue around my dry lips and staggered unsteadily down the path, feeling their eyes measure my wobbly gait. My legs were carrying me just the way

I'd carried those helpless chickens—right down to certain catastrophe.

Mrs. Gunderson stepped out of the house, tying the strings on a clean white apron as I reached the corner of the porch. "Aren't you going to ask these two gentlemen in?" she prodded her husband.

Mr. Gunderson gave a grunt and stood back to motion us all inside. The sharp smell of singed chickens met me at the door, and through a bleary haze I saw Jake look up from the kitchen table and throw me a questioning glance.

"Caught us at a busy time," Mrs. Gunderson fluttered, hurrying us through the kitchen. "All these chickens to be butchered." The stranger grunted a sort of half apology for interrupting, but Mr. Wolverton remained tight-lipped, keeping his angry eyes focused on me.

Once in the sitting room, Mr. Gunderson lowered his thin frame into the cushiony brown armchair and motioned the others to the sofa. I stopped just inside the door.

"Come in, boy," Mr. Gunderson ordered.

I straggled closer. There wasn't anywhere to sit except between the two men on the sofa. I stood, leaning my weight on one leg.

The schoolmaster cleared his throat. He'd removed his hat, and I could see a little blue vein throbbing under the white skin of his temple. "This is Oliver Johnson, Leroy's father," he said.

Both men were glaring at me, and I knew from Mr. Johnson's red-flushed face that Leroy had told them how I'd tricked him. I bit my lip and shifted my weight to the other foot.

Mr. Johnson glared at me. "My son came home from school yesterday with bruises all over his body," he declared. His eyes bored into mine, every word popping like a bullet. "Told me you'd taken him down to the horse barn and beaten him up."

"I saw you slinking out of the barn!" Mr. Wolverton broke in, his face darkening to a purple rage. "Called out to you, but you ran like a coward!"

I tried to take in their words, but I couldn't even swallow, the muscles in my throat were so tight.

"I've had no such trouble in my school before," Mr. Wolverton went on. "What gives you the right, an *orphan* who ought to be grateful everyone's treated you so kindly, to come out here and vent your miserable envy on unsuspecting farm boys?"

I tried to speak, but my tongue wouldn't work at all. I was guilty—but not the way they said! How could I begin to explain, now, that I was sorry? That I'd never meant Leroy any harm?

Mr. Gunderson fixed me with such a cold stare that any thoughts of defending myself went clean out of my head.

"Uh-huh!" the schoolmaster gloated with a satisfied nod. "He has no answer. At least he's wise enough not to try to lie his way out of it." He glanced at Mr. Johnson for approval.

Leroy's father looked away as if sickened by the miserable sight of me.

"Well then," Mr. Wolverton proceeded, "I am going to deal with this infraction so that it will not be repeated. You, boy, will be responsible for keeping the horse barn clean all year. You will shovel out the manure every day after school and put down fresh straw."

He narrowed his gaze. "I will deliver a whipping to you Monday morning in the presence of the other students. I'll let them know you like to use your cowardly fists on smaller children and that any repeated infraction should be immediately reported to me."

Then the schoolmaster smiled, his lips thinning in a tight blue line. "But there will, of course, be no repeated infractions. You will apologize to Leroy Johnson in my hearing, and if you ever lay a hand on one of your younger schoolmates again, you will be expelled."

He glanced at Mr. Gunderson as if making sure he had heard. Mr. Gunderson's eyes never left my face. They were as cold and steely as rifle barrels.

A few seconds later the two men rose to leave. We followed them to the kitchen. As soon as the door closed behind them, Mr. Gunderson turned back to me. He bent down, his eyes square in front of mine. "My son Gus may not have been cut out to be a farmer, but he never gave me any reason to punish him for unseemly behavior!" His breath was hot and sour. "He understood such shenanigans would not be tolerated! I want a full explanation of why you did such a thing! Right now I'm hungry and I've got chickens to deliver. But tonight we will finish this discussion out behind the barn!"

He straightened, and I lifted my chin to follow his eyes, not daring to look away.

"Now," he finished, his voice rising as if he was near to exploding, "you go outside, find Jake, and help with whatever he's doing, and when I see you again, you be ready to talk to me."

I nodded, fumbled with the door, and slipped out to the porch. There, I grabbed hold of a round white pillar to steady myself and clear my head.

Mr. Gunderson's voice followed me through the kitchen window. "Are you satisfied now? Ungrateful little whelp comes out here and beats up an innocent child!"

"I'm not disagreeing with you, Delton," Mrs. Gunderson answered. "You're a good man. I know you're doing your best. Your father whupped you when you needed it and you're only doing the same. I'm just surprised I misjudged the boy so. I never guessed he had a mean streak."

"You have to wonder what's wrong with a boy gets a chance like this and then tears into the first kid that happens to get in his way. I've a good mind to write that Blake fella and tell him what kind of a job he's doing, turning out kids like this!"

"I don't know why he'd do such a thing," she said in a tired voice. "Life is hard enough as it is."

"Life is hard when you're soft, Etta," he reminded her. "Meet hard with harder and you keep things in line."

"I know you're right, Delton," she answered, her voice resigned and wistful. As if she had met hard over and over and it had wounded her deeper every time.

One More Mistake

I slipped off the porch as quietly as I could and trudged out to where Jake was working on the pump below the windmill. He glanced quickly at me and set down his pliers. "Come here," he said gruffly. "We need some tools from the barn."

I trailed him like a puppy.

Jake stepped into the front part of the barn where they kept the small hand tools and harness. He glanced around at the hanging tools, but didn't seem to find what he wanted. Instead, he turned and leaned against the rough wall, facing me.

"You got trouble, boy?" he asked gently.

That's when the sobs came shuddering up my throat. My shoulders shook and my nose took to running.

I must have been a miserable sight—Jake grabbed

me and wrapped his arms roughly around my shoulders. They felt warm and solid, and I cried harder.

Jake didn't speak. I felt him tighten up, but he didn't let go.

When my tears finally dried, I drew a couple of shaky breaths and straightened my spine. Jake let his arms fall, giving me one final rub with his meaty hand before he stuffed both fists in his overalls pockets.

"I never done what they said," I mumbled.

Jake's eyes roved over my face and then away to the rows of harness and tools. "Why'd you run from the school barn?"

"I saw Mr. Wolverton coming and I got scared." The whole awful memory of what I had done and what I had seen washed over me, and guilt stung like barbs all through my gut.

Jake sighed. "You better tell it from the beginning."

I nodded, my chin brushing my chest. I started slowly at what seemed like the beginning, with Pete calling me over at lunch. Jake listened, his face expressionless. It made me think again how different he was from his brother. Jake was as quiet and cool as the barn shadows, while Mr. Gunderson was hot as the glaring sun.

Listening to my own voice, it seemed my thinking

the day before was as full of holes as a sieve. Why had I ever agreed to go along with Pete's plan?

Jake took a deep breath when I was finished. He let it out slow, his troubled eyes moving across my face to see if I'd left out any part. They made me think of Mrs. Gunderson's fingers searching for pinfeathers.

"Well, we've got to tell Delton," he said at last.

I scuffed at the dirt of the barn floor. I wondered could I run off to Crosby and stow away on the train somehow, back to St. Paul?

"It's the hardest part, the telling," Jake said, as if he could read my thoughts. "After that we'll figure what to do and it will get better."

I looked up at him, at his bald mushroom head with the little fringe running around the back, trying to take in what he was saying. "We'll figure what to do," he'd said, words that were like a rope thrown to a drowning man.

I hung on to them and to the feeling of his solid figure striding behind me to the house, where Mr. Gunderson was just finishing lunch. Otherwise I don't know that I'd ever have been able to tell Mr. Gunderson the whole complicated story. But somehow, with Jake standing behind me, I did it.

Mr. Gunderson stared at me in disbelief, as if I'd surely concocted the whole tale out there in the barn.

I didn't blame him. The second telling made it sound even less likely than the first.

"You blaming Pete and Mike, those other two, for getting you into this scrape, boy?" he snorted when I'd finished what I had to say.

I shrank back from his question, clutching the edge of the table where the Missus went on cutting and clawing out the chicken entrails as she listened, her hands and wrists stained bloodred.

"No, sir," I declared grimly, shaking my head.

"You're just as guilty as if you'd beat him up with your fists, leading him into that barn!"

"Yes, sir." He was right. I had to admit it.

"I don't have much truck with those that can't keep out of trouble," Mr. Gunderson went on flatly. "Don't see as how with the little you do it's worth keepin' you here."

Mrs. Gunderson's hands stopped midstroke. I stared straight ahead, not daring to breathe. The only sound was the gentle sigh of the wind through the curtains of the open kitchen window.

Mr. Gunderson shot Jake a steady look, as if making sure he was paying attention, before he finished with me. "I'm thinkin' I'll write a letter to the orphanage today. Let 'em know I'm sending him back. Not that much work here in the winter anyway."

My eyes clouded. The world spun black. The smell of warm chicken guts rolled in over my dazed senses, and without warning my knees gave a lurch. I grabbed the table quick to keep them from buckling. Jake's hand shot out to steady me.

"You can't do that," I heard him say. I thought at first he meant my toppling over.

Mr. Gunderson stared back at Jake as if he were a plucked chicken that had just sat up and demanded his feathers back.

Jake let his hand fall and cleared his throat. "You can't just send the boy back for a trick that was pulled on him in school," he declared.

"He's trouble!" Mr. Gunderson roared with an angry wave of his hand. "I don't need no borrowed trouble—I got trouble enough already!"

"You said you'd have him for the year," Jake stammered.

I blinked hard. I would not cry again.

"*They* told *me* no more 'n a year 'less I adopted him." Mr. Gunderson gave a little snarl like he was hurling Jake's misunderstanding back in his face. "They sure couldn't force a man to keep a boy here after he'd proved to be a liar and a troublemaker."

"All right, then," Jake said. I heard him step back toward the door, retreating. Why he had bothered to try to change his brother's mind, I couldn't guess. He'd known him centuries before I had, and I already knew that what Mr. Gunderson said was as good as done as soon as it passed his lips.

"*I'll* take him for the rest of the year," Jake stated, his voice quiet but sure.

My whole body shook as a shock wave rippled through it.

"*You'll* take him!" Mr. Gunderson flung back, his voice thick with disbelief. The Missus dropped her butcher knife. It clattered across the floor. Her husband seemed not to hear it. "And keep him where?" he demanded.

"He can stay with me. In my house," Jake declared.

"Now, Delton, there's really no need—" Mrs. Gunderson started to say.

But he cut her off. "Yes, there is!" he thundered. "Yes, we'll move him out, by God. You want 'im, Jake? You want an orphan? All right, by God, you got him! And don't think I won't write a letter this very night telling that highfalutin orphan overseer what I think of him and his operation!"

My arms and legs started shaking, and I bit down on my bottom lip to stop its quivering. "He's Jake's now, you hear that?" Mr. Gunderson raved, pacing back and forth. "Jake's orphan." Then he stopped and pointed a stern finger at me. "Unless there's even one more mistake. *Even one!* You do anything out of line, I send you right back. Jake wants the bother of putting up with you, that's his nonsense. But I'm the one's got my name on the agreement. *I stay in charge!*"

With that Mr. Gunderson shot Jake one more solid glare and stomped from the room, making the very walls tremble as he passed.

We stood, the three of us, in a sort of dumbstruck shock of disbelief, none of us looking at the others. After a minute Mrs. Gunderson wiped her hands on her apron, marched resolutely to the cupboard, and brought down three glasses. "I think I'll just draw us all up some nice buttermilk," she stated, as if she were announcing afternoon teatime in a society house.

I watched her march out the kitchen door to go around to the outside cellar steps.

"Jake," I croaked, "Jake . . . " But I couldn't put my tongue to the words that were somersaulting in my mind.

He looked at me the way he had the first day, and I knew he was reading all I couldn't say. Then his smooth face wrinkled into a broad grin. "Wait'll she sees she wiped her bloody hands on her best company-come-a-callin' apron."

I grinned and choked out a strangled kind of cry before I bolted across the kitchen floor and flung my arms around Jake's waist. I hugged him hard for a moment before I turned and escaped out the door.

I galloped down to the pasture, not knowing where to go except away, by myself. The sweet-smelling prairie air filled my lungs the way the boundless blue majesty of the sky filled my eyes. It was all so big, too big to take in and hold on to. And so open. Open and warm as the smiling autumn sunlight. It felt as though I only had to be there, to breathe the prairie in and gaze it in, and it would fill me with the wholeness of itself.

Mr. Gunderson's words were still banging around in my head. . . . "If there's even one more mistake I send you right back. . . ." But then my mind started playing another voice—Jake's. "*I'll* take him," he'd said.

"*I'll take him.*"

I took to whooping and hollering and laughing. It was as close as a boy like me could come to warbling out a song of joy. I whirled and danced and cackled until I fell in a giggling heap, rolling down the hill, letting the grass and flowers tickle my ears and face and feeling a part of the bugs and worms and butter-flies and glad, just glad, to be one more creature on the good warm earth. It was a prairie joy dance, all mixed with the endless shuffling grass underneath, the riffling clouds overhead, and the critters burrow-ing and creeping and cavorting in between.

It felt—in spite of what Mr. Gunderson had warned me—it felt as if I'd come home.

Jake's House

J ake saddled Babe and disappeared that afternoon. He was gone until milking time.

After Mr. Gunderson loaded the chickens in the flivver and drove down the driveway in a cloud of dust, the Missus helped me move my things out to Jake's house. I hung my spare clothes on a peg behind the door before turning around to survey the single room. It smelled softly of Jake's sweat and lye soap and kerosene. There was a cot that folded down from the wall for Jake's bed and a small black iron stove. A table with a kerosene lantern on it stood with two chairs in the middle of the room. The only thing on the walls besides the clothes pegs was a towel roller nailed to the inside of the door and a hunting rifle laid across two spikes in the wall.

Mrs. Gunderson stopped just inside the threshold, my sheets and blanket in her arms. She looked around and gave a sniff of disapproval. Then she sighed and laid the bedding on the table with a little shake of her head. I didn't know where the sheets ought to go either, but I supposed they'd have to be laid on the floor.

"Take this," she said when she returned, puffing, from another trip to the house. She carried a coarse rag rug, which she said could be spread out as a sort of mattress.

"Now," she asserted when I'd set the rolled rug on the floor next to Jake's bed, "you'd best take the wheelbarrow and finish digging my potatoes so the whole afternoon don't go to waste."

Still, she put out a hand to stop me as I scuttled toward the door. Reaching to scoop the hair back out of my eyes, she peered into my face. "You do your best to stay out of trouble, hear?" she said gruffly.

I nodded, not sure how to answer.

"It's a hard country," she went on, her gray eyes leaving me and roving over Jake's cot and stove once more. "Not a fit country for a woman to stay in and keep her sanity." She seemed not to be speaking to me anymore, but to someone inside her. Her eyes had narrowed, focused on some far-off point, and I don't think she knew how deep her fingers dug into my arm.

"Only the strong can survive here," she whispered.

"Some folks'd sell their soul to hang on to this land, but it has a heart of stone. Some years it's hail. Or grasshoppers. Or the sun, just baking everything to powder."

She blinked then and seemed to remember herself and loosened her grip. "Try to stay out of trouble," she repeated. But I could tell she didn't think I stood a chance of doing it, the way I aggravated Mr. Gunderson so easy. "My husband is a hard man," she said when I hesitated, "but he's hardest of all on himself. He doesn't want another son. Not another disappointment. Gus was never strong enough for farming. He was a good boy, always obedient, which was why, of course, well, it made it hard for him to decide to go, knowing how his father felt about this place. But he is our son. He's Delton's son and no one could be . . . you never could be that. Don't blame yourself."

I kept my eyes on her face another moment, feeling her words try to soak into my stubborn skin. They were harsh words, but not meant to be unkind. Still, I wanted to shake them off, like a dog just coming out of the water. I shrugged out of her grasp, past her rumpled, soft body and out the door.

That evening Mr. Gunderson, Jake, and I did the milking with the least words possible, which were mighty few.

When we filed in to supper there was a sealed letter propped up on the table waiting to be mailed. The
words *St. Paul Orphanage* jumped off the paper at me.
Jake eyed the envelope, too, as though he wondered if
it might burst into flame with the heated words Mr.
Gunderson probably had written inside. I tried to
imagine what Mr. Blake would think, what he'd tell
Acorn. I wondered if they'd both understand that I
would most likely be following close behind the letter, as little time as it would take me to make one
more mistake.

Mrs. Gunderson set a steaming pot of chicken and
dumplings in front of us, and we bowed our heads
while she offered her usual blessing before we lit into
the food. It was a revelation to me how many noises
four people made with their clanking silverware and
their creaking chairs when there were no words hov-
ering in the air.

Jake stared pointedly at the envelope as he
chewed. Mrs. Gunderson followed his eyes and tact-
fully dropped hers again to her plate. Mr. Gunderson
trailed Jake's gaze with a glare and a frown before he
cleared his throat and said, "I wrote, like I said I
would."

I peeked at Jake out of the corner of my eye. His

face was as still as pond water. He didn't even grunt in response.

In a moment Mr. Gunderson spoke again. "You planning to finish greasing that windmill tomorrow?"

"Figured there'd be plenty of time," Jake answered.

"Be time to break up that bottom land before the snow flies."

"Yep," Jake agreed. After that everyone shifted in their chairs and seemed to eat a little cheerier, as if the men's words had pushed back the uneasy silence.

After supper Mr. Gunderson ambled into the sitting room to listen to the news on the wireless.

Mrs. Gunderson turned from the sink as Jake and I got up from the table. "I sent a rug for the boy to sleep on," she said quietly to Jake. "Don't know where you'll store the bedding."

Jake glanced at her and then quickly away. "We'll manage," he said. He stepped to the door, then seemed to remember something and turned to look back at her. "Thanks, Etta," he said.

She took a breath as if to answer, but Jake was already gone.

I followed him across the yard to his house. The kerosene lamp bathed the little shack in a warm glow. Jake doubled the rug over to make an extra thickness and laid it beside the longest wall, at right angles to his bed. In the lantern light it looked to be the coziest room in the world. I found the book I'd brought down from the house and carried it over to the table.

Jake looked up from a sock he was darning.

"Went to talk to Leroy Johnson," he said casually. I stared at him. "Told him what you'd said, and he admitted to what they'd done."

I figured that by "they" Jake meant Pete and Mike.

"Oliver Johnson seems a fair enough man. He rode over with me to speak to the schoolmaster."

I gasped. "You talked to Mr. Wolverton?"

"He'll meet with those two boys' parents tomorrow," Jake said. "Punishment will be the same as before. Only it will be the three of you doing it."

My heart sank. Pete and Mike would be furious that I'd told.

"You be wary of those two, you hear?" Jake advised me, his voice firm but kindly.

I met his eyes again and nodded slowly.

His face softened into little smile crinkles. "Mr. Wolverton thought it best to tell those boys he'd spotted 'em leaving the school barn riding the same horse."

I let out my breath in relief. "He said that? He said he'd tell them that?" I asked, just to hear it for sure.

"He said that's how he remembered it, once he

thought it over," Jake replied, turning sober again. But his eyes danced. "Just coincidentally that's how Leroy happened to mention they left, too." Jake lifted his sock back up to the light and jabbed the needle through.

I went back to my book, trying to look as busy as Jake did and biting my lip to keep from busting out laughing. Jake had told the schoolmaster the whole story all right, and even nudged him to concoct one of his own to keep Pete and Mike from suspecting I'd spilled the beans. I was lucky, and powerfully grateful, to have Jake stick up for me the way he had.

In the gentle quiet of Jake's little shack I got to thinking of my brother again. Had Acorn ever once met a man like Jake? Someone who would stand up for him for no reason but plain kindness? I shut my eyes tight, locking out *that* thought. But I couldn't shut out another—I hadn't written Acorn a letter to let him know I still remembered my promise. If I knew Acorn, he'd be wondering why I hadn't sent for him yet. But how could I tell him the truth: that I hadn't even asked if he could come. That nobody here cared that I had a brother—one more nuisance to put up with; one more ungrateful orphan who'd get himself in more trouble than Mr. Gunderson could notch on his belt.

The day I left Acorn, I'd told myself it was only for a little while. I'd made a promise and I'd intended to keep it. But I was probably further away now than I'd ever been from sending for my brother. Maybe Acorn had seen the truth that last day when I refused to. Maybe he'd known how it was going to be—that the distance between us would work like a mighty wedge. And time, weighing it down, would only widen the gap. There wasn't any hope, really, that we'd ever be together again until Mr. Gunderson sent me back to the orphanage to stay.

Taking a Chance

The following week winter arrived with a blast of cold and snow. The Missus lamented that we'd never gotten the barn painted, and Mr. Gunderson and Jake had to ride out in the whirling snow and bring the cows in to the shelter of the corral behind the barn. But mostly things went on pretty much the same as ever except that I spent the evenings in Jake's house. In the mornings my nose felt like ice and I'd huddle stiff and still under the covers until I heard Jake open the stove lid to stir up the coal embers. Then I'd jump up and scramble into my overalls.

I liked it there. I liked waking up at night and hearing the sound of Jake's breathing. Sometimes he snored, once so loud I had to get up and shake his elbow to make him stop. I liked talking to him evenings in the light of the lantern. Jake told me stories about the first people to farm this land and how they'd lived in houses made of sod. He explained things about the cows and the farm and even about the coyotes, when we heard them howl, and about the geese that gabbled overhead in great snowy flocks, winging their way south.

One night when I came in I stopped short. There was Acorn's knife sitting square in the middle of the table, the blade gleaming like a winking eye in the yellow light of the kerosene lamp. I shot a sharp glance at Jake, my heart hammering against my ribs, and was startled to see his eyes watching me closely.

"That little dandy fell out of your bag," he said quietly. "I pulled out your things from under the cot and gave them a shakedown checking for mice. Thought you'd want to know where it was."

"It was my brother's," I said, my face flushing hot. I felt as if Jake had caught me with stolen goods.

Jake cocked his head, still studying me. "You've got a brother?"

I nodded. "Back at the orphanage."

"What did he use it for?" Jake asked casually.

I kept my eyes on the knife, not wanting Jake to read my thoughts. I didn't know what Acorn had hoped to do with the knife and I didn't want to tell

Jake about his runaways and his bank-robbing hobo buddies. "It was a gift from a friend."

"This the only thing you got of his?"

"Yeah," I said, uncertain what he was getting at.

"It's got a fancy handle." Jake picked up the knife and turned it over, admiring the carvings. "It's a fine knife. Somebody put a lot of work into it."

"I'm keeping it for him," I said.

Jake grunted at that, turned it over once more, then handed it to me. "You keeping that barn clean at school?"

"Yes, sir," I assured him. Mr. Wolverton had delivered his promised whipping to Pete and Mike and me the Monday after Jake talked to him. He assigned us each a day to clean the barn, but Pete and Mike usually helped each other out. That's what pals are for, I suppose. I worked alone and it suited me fine. Suited Jake fine, too. He didn't want me spending any more time than necessary hanging out with the two of them.

"Then it's time I took you hunting," Jake declared, snapping my mind back to the little room that was Jake's house. That's what we did, too, the next three or four Saturdays. The best hunting comes after the first snowfall, Jake said. And it *was* good hunting for us. We brought home a buck one day and later a good-size doe.

* * *

One night, late in November, Mrs. Gunderson was humming to herself when Jake and I came in the door for supper. I smelled fried chicken. Jake seemed to scent something else.

"This your birthday, Etta?" he asked, eyeing her quizzically.

She dimpled prettily, waving him away like an old tease. "Just something special I know about," she said. "I'll let Delton tell you."

Jake and I exchanged a mystified glance before Mr. Gunderson put an end to all the nonsense. "Etta's talked me into taking her to Fargo," he said, making it clear that the trip would be a nuisance. "We'll pay Gus a visit and do some shopping. Etta's got her egg money burning a hole in her pocket. Think you can handle the chores?"

Jake looked over at me and frowned. I stared back, waiting. Then he turned his frown to the Missus, whose smile faded, watching him. "The boy and me will starve without a cook," Jake stated.

Mrs. Gunderson's jaw dropped for just a second

before she suddenly chuckled and picked up a biscuit to fire at him. Jake caught it just before it hit his chest. He grinned back at her.

Mr. Gunderson muttered something, shaking his head, and pulled out his chair.

"I'll make you doughnuts and have everything laid out for you," she fussed as she set the chicken on the table and turned back to get the gravy pan out of the warming oven. "You'd think I was leaving for a month!" But she wasn't really angry; she was laughing in spite of herself when she sat down at the table. Jake cupped his chin in his hand to cover his smile and she glanced at him, then at her husband, who had just reached for the chicken, ignoring the foolishness around him. The Missus sobered then, but not before she flicked a potholder at Jake as if to snuff out his teasing.

"Go ahead. Stay a month," Jake said, passing me the potatoes. "We can handle everything."

"Won't be no month," Mr. Gunderson answered. "We'll leave on the Monday afternoon train and be back again next Monday. That's enough shopping time, right?"

The Missus cocked her chin, turned to glance at the teapot where she always tucked her egg money, and then nodded. I watched her, thinking I'd never seen her so excited or so pretty. I wondered which made her happier, the chance to see Gus or the shopping time.

By Monday morning I had gotten caught up in the excitement of seeing the Gundersons go. Jake made it sound like it would be a holiday for us, having the place to ourselves. "Could be it's time you showed me how to drive that flivver down the road," Jake told Mr. Gunderson at breakfast.

"Could be it's time for you, but it ain't time for the flivver," Mr. Gunderson replied dryly. "The road north of here's blocked with snow, and besides, I drained the radiator."

"Humph," Jake replied. He'd never taken much interest before in the flivver or what went on with its radiator and such. Mr. Gunderson seemed to be thinking the same thing. He studied his brother for a long moment before he buttered himself another slice of toast.

I was gone to school when Jake delivered the Gundersons to the train in Crosby. We moved into the main house that night because it was foolish to heat two houses. I moved my clothes and bedding back into Gus's old room and was surprised at how plain and cold it was, as if the frosty windowpane was useless to keep out the winter in spite of the kitchen grate. That first night I dreamed the fields were on fire again and woke up shaking in a cold sweat. I realized the last time I'd dreamed of fires was the first night I slept in Jake's house. I'd bolted up in bed, trying not to scream and staring around blindly, not sure where I was. Then I'd heard the sound of Jake's steady breathing and settled back down, remembering how I'd come to be there. That memory settled me again. Jake was right downstairs.

The week went by fast. Every day, I hurried home as quick as I could from school. On Friday Jake was waiting for me at the barn with a mischievous glint in his eye. "I left you some of Etta's cookies on the table," he reported cheerfully. "Grab 'em quick and come back down here."

I did as I was told. Chores didn't seem like chores with Mr. Gunderson gone. The front door of the barn was closed against the wind, and I trotted around to the back.

There was a yelp and a rustle as a gold-and-white bundle of fur shot out and threw itself against my legs. I fell to my knees to snatch up the puppy, but it wriggled out of my reach. Jake's grin was as broad as the barn door in which he stood.

"From Al," he said simply. "Buddy had pups, and he came by with one for you."

"For me?" I echoed joyfully. "You think it will be all right with Mr. Gunderson?"

Jake sobered and shrugged. "Guess she's already here," he said.

"Thanks, Jake," I breathed.

Jake's smile danced out across his face again. "She's a female. Best of the litter."

"You pick her out?"

Jake gave one short nod. "Over a month ago. Al wanted you to have first pick."

It made me glad to think Jake and Al had planned this surprise for so long. The puppy licked my face and let me grab her for a moment before she wiggled free again.

"Got a name for her?" Jake prodded.

I thought about a name. Then I remembered the cows' names and Mr. Gunderson's disgust. "Think I'll just call her Pup."

"You ponder on it, the right name will come to you," Jake said before he turned back to the barn.

I snapped my fingers and the puppy cocked her head and looked at me, her bright eyes snapping with curiosity. I realized Jake was right—a smart pup like this one deserved a name. Likely she'd come expecting one, along with her new home. And it was right that I should name her, since she'd been put in my care. Still, it would take me time to think about it. I wanted the name to be just right.

I guess I was thinking how this time, for sure, I wouldn't write down her name where just anyone could see it. Jake had taken a chance, agreeing to bring her home without checking with his brother. One thing I knew if I knew anything—Delton Gunderson wouldn't be pleased to come home to any surprises.

An Unexpected Visitor

Saturday morning Jake and I ground oats. It was a dusty job, powdering our eyelashes and clothes and the cold interior of the barn with a gray film. We tied the pup outside, and every time we shut down the grinder between loads I heard her crying to be let in.

It was time for lunch when we finished putting away grain shovels and buckets. We were heading up to the house, my pup at our heels, when we heard the clop-clop of horse hooves on the hard snow. A wagon turned into the yard.

"Helloo!" the driver hailed us, pulling the team to a stop.

"Charlie Anderson!" Jake called, recognizing our neighbor to the south. The pup gave a yip and dashed toward the newcomers.

"Got a passenger for you!" Anderson said, jerking

his head to the boy seated beside him. "Came in on the train. Nobody there to meet him."

Jake frowned and strode forward. I followed, a funny feeling gnawing in my gut. The boy wore a woolen cap with flaps over his ears, and he'd tied a thick scarf around the turned-up collar of his coat. He sat perfectly still.

"Can't be for us," Jake was saying as he reached the wagon. "We're not expecting anybody here."

Anderson glanced in surprise at his passenger. "Told me clear as day he was supposed to . . ."

I didn't hear the rest. I'd come up close enough to see the face. That firm-set mouth, the chin, those freckles. I knew in a rush of plain astonishment that I was looking at my brother.

Acorn suddenly grinned and threw off the lap robe, leaping up.

"Acorn?" I half whispered, thinking he might disappear in a *poof!* of smoke if I spoke too loud. "Acorn!" I said again, stepping forward in a kind of daze and grabbing him as he scrambled down over the wheel.

I saw Jake's face—a look of pure puzzlement—before Acorn wrapped his arms around my neck and spun me in a circle.

Mr. Anderson wasted no time climbing over the

back of the seat and handing my brother's bag down to Jake. "Wasn't any trouble, seeing your place was right on my way," he said cheerfully.

The little pup was yipping like crazy now, circling Acorn and me and then darting over to challenge Anderson's horses. Our neighbor picked up the reins and gave a wave as he drove away.

I stepped back to get a good look at the grinning face of my brother. It seemed my heart might bust at the sight of him. I couldn't even think what to say.

"Guess you two know each other," Jake drawled from behind me.

I dropped my arm from Acorn's shoulder and turned around slow. "He's my brother," I said. My own words were almost like news to me, too—as if they woke me up to think how complicated Acorn's coming would be.

Jake put out his hand.

Acorn grabbed it in his mittened paw and shook hard. He was a sight, all bundled up in an oversize coat with sleeves so long they bunched where he'd pushed them back at the wrists. "Pleasetameetya," Acorn said. Then we all three stood looking at one another so quiet even the pup stopped her yapping and sat down on her haunches to stare at us.

It took a minute for me to realize Jake was watch-

ing me, giving me leave to ask the first questions.
Acorn's eyes were planted on me, too. "How did you
get here?" I finally asked. "How did you know where I
was?"

"Mr. Blake told me," Acorn answered quickly.

The disbelief must have shown on my face. "Mr.
Blake *sent* you here?"

Acorn's eyes dropped just for an instant. Then he
seemed to decide he might as well tell the truth and
get it over with. "I hopped a freight," he said. "He
don't know I come here."

"But you said—"

"He *told* me 'cause I kept askin' him," Acorn
butted in, fixing me with a look that made me let him
finish. "Every day I'd ask him and every day he'd tell
me a little more. Finally he got a map and showed me
where you'd gone. Showed me the dot for the town
marked Crosby. He even let me keep the map."

I kept my eyes on Acorn's, taking in his words.
"Every day I asked him. . . ." Acorn had pestered Mr.
Blake *every day*.

"So they don't know where you run off to?" Jake's
voice broke into my whirling thoughts.

"No, sir," Acorn answered solemnly.

Jake glanced at me again. "Guess we better go in
and get cleaned up," he said. "Bet you're hungry," he

added, looking at Acorn. He picked up my brother's bag.

Acorn's eyes were as big and round as brass knobs when he saw the lunch Jake set out. He wolfed down a thick slice of Mrs. Gunderson's white bread and stared when he saw the plate of cold cuts Jake brought out for sandwiches. Acorn saved the canned peaches for last once he saw we each got our own bowlful. I couldn't help grinning when I set out a plate of molasses cookies and the doughnuts the Missus had made special when she left. Anyone could see my brother hadn't eaten in a while. Jake must have noticed, but he didn't say a word about it. Just, "Why don't you show him where to put his things?" to me when we were finished eating.

I looked at Jake, my eyes full of questions, I suppose.

"Nothing to be decided till Monday," he said, giving me a little smile. "You go on; I'll clean up here."

I led the way upstairs to Gus's room with the pup scrambling at our heels.

"Doesn't he ever decide anything until Mondays?" Acorn asked me when we were alone.

I looked at him, suddenly realizing how little Acorn understood the mess he'd made for everyone. "That's the day the Gundersons come back," I said.

"Who's *he?*" Acorn asked, jabbing a finger toward the floor grate.

I sighed and tried to think where to begin. I explained about there being two Gunderson brothers and where Mr. and Mrs. Gunderson had gone. I'd barely started when I realized Acorn had lost interest. He was gazing around him, taking in the room the way I had that first day. He looked as curious as the puppy, who was sniffing the covers of the unmade bed, poking the rungs of the single wooden chair, and burying her nose in the woven rag rug.

Acorn snapped his fingers at the collie pup. "What's her name?" he asked.

I shrugged. "Just got her yesterday," I said, though it seemed as if it had been weeks ago.

"So she's yours, then?" Acorn asked, impressed.

"Yeah."

Acorn bounced down on the bed. "You got us a nice place here," he said. His words cut straight to my heart. How could I even begin to tell him the way things really were with the Gundersons? The truth would snuff out all that shine in his eyes, and I couldn't bear it.

"Mr. Blake said you asked the Gundersons to take me with you when you left," Acorn told me, growing serious. "He told me not to take it to heart, me losin' a brother."

So Mr. Blake had tried to smooth over my leaving. I was grateful for that. I kept my eyes on Acorn's face, feeling sorry and guilty and . . . scared.

"I told you to wait for me," I said, trying to keep my voice light. "Why didn't you do what I said?"

Acorn shot me a look of surprise. "I *did* wait!" he declared. "I waited way longer than you said. And they lost your letters. Mrs. Mercer said that happens all the time. She kept an eye out for 'em, too."

My heart sort of crumpled as I pictured Mrs. Mercer searching in her mailbag every time Acorn asked if there was a letter from me.

"So I thought I'd better come looking," Acorn continued. "Mr. Pearson drew a line on the map for me in geography class, so I knew which way to go. I hopped a freight to Fargo and met some fellas there who told me how to get to Carrington and then on to Minot. I stayed out of sight and only talked to the bums out in the yards. They were glad to help."

I couldn't even imagine how Acorn had come all that way hitching rides on and off freight trains. How could I tell him, when he'd come so far, that things were nothing like he thought? I didn't have a place ready for him. Mr. Gunderson would . . . I had to close my eyes tight to try to shut out the image of Mr. Gunderson's face when he saw Acorn.

Two of us! Two! And he wanted to be rid of the one.

When I opened my eyes again, Acorn had slid down to the floor, where the puppy could lick his face. He wrapped his arms around her, then giggled as her long tongue lapped the back of his neck. "I think you should call her Lady," he said.

I smiled grimly. I knew I had to tell him the truth.

"Acorn," I said quietly, thinking of Jake in the kitchen and my voice through the grate, "I haven't asked the Gundersons again to let you come here. Mr. Gunderson was always so mad at me, there wasn't ever a good time. He wrote to Mr. Blake about me. He'll send you back, Acorn, soon as he gets home."

Acorn's eyes clouded. He pushed the pup away. "I won't go back," he declared.

"You can't stay here if you're not wanted," I shot back, and was immediately sorry I'd been so hard. "They'll send us both back," I added then, feeling the sharp knife edge of my words slicing me deep inside.

"I don't need this place," my brother stated. "Nobody has to worry about lookin' after me but me. I look after myself."

His ten-year-old bluster made me tired. "Listen to me, Acorn—"

"I decided after they sent you away that I could take care of myself. It's not like I expected anything comin' here, Tree. I'm out of the orphanage, that's all I care about. Where I go next don't matter at all."

"All right," I said, seeing I was as useless as ever at making him look at things any way but his. "It don't matter what happens Monday, then. Just you be polite, you hear me? Mrs. Gunderson's real nice. And Jake has stood up for me. Mr. Gunderson is hard, but he's been fair. These people don't put stock in rough manners. Will you be polite with them, at least?"

Acorn was watching me with a suspicious look in his eye. Still, he nodded at my question.

"All right," I said again. "Maybe they'll see you had good intentions. Maybe they'll take some time to think it over." Maybe there'll be a miracle from heaven, I could have said. "You just act real nice. And I'll vouch for what a hard worker you are," I added. It was easy to promise. Nobody'd be interested in my two cents worth anyhow.

"Don't you think they'll know that, bein' I'm your brother?" he asked me.

I looked at Acorn and saw something that I'd forgotten: that fierce, burning sort of look he had. And something else. When I left him, Acorn and I had seemed like two ends of a rope that had stretched to the limit the farther away I went. But now, it was as if we'd suddenly snapped back together. Being brothers, we were tangled together—and always would be—the way roots are, and branches, too.

I couldn't blame Acorn for coming after me any more than I could blame my mother for the fire that took her away. But when the Gundersons came home, I'd be powerless to make any difference in what they decided. Helpless, that's what I was, just the same as I'd always been.

Wind Rising

Acorn pitched in and helped out with the chores. I tried not to let myself think about Monday, knowing these were probably my last days with Jake. It seemed a hundred years ago when I'd thought the week the Gundersons were gone would be a holiday for the two of us.

Jake sat me down Saturday night while Acorn ran outside with the puppy. He had been watching me all day, and I knew he saw the worry in my face. "Try to let it rest until Monday," he told me. "No sense borrowing trouble. One good thing," he added when Acorn pushed open the door and the puppy came bounding into the kitchen, "now that your brother's here, Delton will hardly notice the pup."

That made me smile. But it didn't stop the worry eating away at my insides.

✳ ✳ ✳

Monday dawned as regular as any other day. Jake sent Acorn along with me to school. "Delton and Etta will be back by the time you get home," he reminded me as Acorn tramped ahead out the door, eager to be off. I stood with my hand on the knob, looking back at Jake. I knew he was warning me that everything could change when they got here. It was as though he was saying good-bye without really saying it because . . . well, because we each had ourselves our own brother to think about.

At school all the kids gathered around to have a look at Acorn. I didn't tell them he was my brother, not wanting to explain why he hadn't come with me in the first place. How could I say the Gundersons hadn't wanted him?

"So you're an orphan, just like him?" Leroy Johnson asked. My brother turned questioning eyes at me.

"That's right," I said, looking away. All I could think about was what the Gundersons would say when we got home from school.

It was a long day. Once, Mr. Wolverton asked me a question and I stared back at him without a clue to what he'd said.

"North America!" Helen whispered from across the aisle.

"North America!" I said, aloud.

Mr. Wolverton nodded, and I shot Helen a grateful look. She gave me a quick smile, then dropped her eyes to her papers.

✳ ✳ ✳

The pup bounded out past the tree rows to meet us when we came across the field after school. "Lady! Lady!" Acorn shouted gleefully, dropping the book Mr. Wolverton had let him take home and clasping his arms around the collie while they rolled in the snow. I saw the wagon pulled up at the house, so I knew the Gundersons must have just arrived. I wondered how Jake had explained the puppy.

I made her stay on the porch and followed my brother into the kitchen. They were all there, Jake and Mr. and Mrs. Gunderson. She looked up and smiled at me, her face flushed from bending to poke coal into the range. Mr. Gunderson was seated at the table as if he'd pulled out a chair to visit with Jake.

"What's this?" he rumbled, his eyes falling on Acorn.

I looked at Jake, feeling a jolt of something like hurt, I guess, that he hadn't at least warned them.

"It's the boy's brother," Jake said evenly. "He came on the train."

"From *Minnesota?*" Mr. Gunderson shot me a quick glance, his bushy eyebrows knotting together in a frown.

I opened my mouth to try to explain, when Acorn stepped forward. "I come on my own, sir," he said. "Nobody sent for me." I could see my brother figured he knew what questions were next.

Mr. Gunderson fixed him with a stony stare. "You come on your own," he repeated. "You buy yourself a ticket?"

"No, sir," Acorn answered promptly. "I hopped a freight, sir."

Mr. Gunderson straightened as if he found it hard to believe a kid Acorn's size could do such a thing. "You ran away?"

Acorn hesitated, then nodded slowly.

"Got people back there lookin' for you—wonderin' where you went?" Mr. Gunderson demanded. I could tell it irritated him, thinking a worthless orphan had managed to make such a nuisance of himself.

Acorn wet his lips. "I couldn't leave 'em a note,

sir. Couldn't run the chance they'd catch up to me 'fore I got out of town."

Mr. Gunderson glowered at Acorn like he was a rat he'd caught slipping into the henhouse. "How old are you, ten?"

"I'm almost eleven, sir."

"Almost eleven," Mr. Gunderson nodded grimly once or twice, as though he was adding up all the things Acorn had told him. "All right," he said solidly, coming to a decision. "You just turn right around and hop on a freight headin' back where you come from. We got no place for you here."

I caught my breath, watching Acorn's back stiffen at Mr. Gunderson's words. I remembered how I'd told him I'd vouch for what a worker he was, and I tried to think how to say it, but my brain just wouldn't work. I opened my mouth, taking a good breath to speak out, but my voice wouldn't come. My silence shamed me, but I also knew my speaking up would only bring Mr. Gunderson's wrath down harder.

I could tell Acorn was getting ready to fire back a retort. Then he hesitated, looking down at his boots, where the snow was melting in little puddles on Mrs. Gunderson's linoleum. I hoped he was thinking, maybe, about how I'd warned him to be polite.

Even so, his words caught me by surprise. "I thank

you for your time, sir," he said as stately as a prince in a fairy tale. "I was really only passin' through." With that Acorn turned and stepped back toward the door, as if he had never even thought of staying. There he turned around again, his chin held high, his face as blank as a new slate. "I'll be needin' my bag from upstairs," he said.

Nobody made a move, we were that caught off guard. I heard the wind pick up outside. There was the sharp *ping! ping!* of ice crystals spatting against the windowpanes and the creak of the roof timbers bracing themselves against the rising gale. Lady whined at the door.

Clang! We all jumped at the sound of Mrs. Gunderson banging a bread pan down hard on the stove. She stood still as everyone turned startled eyes on her. All the time her husband had asked Acorn his questions, she'd held her peace, watching and listening. I thought I'd seen her catch her breath when he suddenly sent Acorn packing, and I'd watched her face soften the minute my brother spoke his princely words. Now she stepped around the table and set her eyes firmly on Acorn's as he stood at the door.

"Storm's coming," she said sternly. "Nobody's going anywhere with the wind picking up like this. You just take off your coats now, both of you. Look at the mess you've made on the floor! I got cocoa ready—warm you all up before you finish unloading the wagon."

Mr. Gunderson turned to stare at her as she set about bringing cups down from the shelf. I unbuttoned my coat and stepped as light as I could to the rug to wipe my boots. Acorn caught my glance, and I was glad to see the sparkle back in his eyes—as if he understood I couldn't have helped any. Watching my brother shrug out of his coat, I was grateful to the wind and Mrs. Gunderson for buying us a little more time.

"The boys can stay in Gus's room for tonight," Mrs. Gunderson declared as she set a plate of cookies in front of her husband and motioned Jake to a chair. "It's too cold out in Jake's house anyway."

Acorn and I came quietly to the table. Mr. Gunderson ignored us, his stormy eyes following the Missus as she set two steaming cups in front of us and turned back to the stove. "What about the dog Jake's brought home? Are you going to dole out sleeping arrangements for her, too?" he demanded.

"She'll be fine in the barn," Jake quickly put in.

Mr. Gunderson glanced at his brother. "Well!" he snorted. Then, after a long moment, "Well, by damn!

I guess everybody's got things planned out so I don't even have to give it a thought! If I'm lucky, nobody's farmed out my own bed while I been gone!"

Nobody answered. We were all much too busy sipping cocoa.

✳ ✳ ✳

Before we came in from milking that night, Jake tied several ropes together to make a long line from the barn door to the porch. That way no one would get lost going to the barn in the morning if there was a raging blizzard.

The wind was whining a lonesome wail when Acorn and I crawled into bed. "It's really blowing out there," I said, hearing the window sashes rattle. I was wondering if it was quieter in Jake's house, where the snow could wrap around and make a bank up past the windows.

"You think Mr. Gunderson will send me out to-morrow if it's as bad as this?" Acorn asked after a minute.

I didn't think even Mr. Gunderson could get away with something as heartless as that, but I didn't want to give my brother false hope. "It'll have blown itself out by morning," I told him.

And in the morning I'd have a different kind of

storm to face. Mr. Gunderson hadn't said *I* had to leave. But even if he didn't send me, how could I let Acorn go off on his own? He'd made it clear he wouldn't ever go back to the orphanage and that meant . . . well, it meant he'd head just anywhere— alone. It was one thing to leave him waiting at the orphanage; it was quite something else to let him go with no way to ever find him again.

But how could I walk away from the only chance I'd ever had of having a home and family? The Gundersons had made it clear they weren't looking for another son, but I wanted to hang on, to stay as long as I could and work as hard as I could, in hopes they'd change their minds.

I lay still, breathing deep and even, so Acorn would think I'd already fallen asleep. I didn't want him asking me what I planned to do when Mr. Gunderson sent him on his way.

When Trains Don't Run

The next morning the wind was still whining and rattling the windows. I jumped out of bed and scraped a peephole through the frost on the glass. All I could make out was a whirling ocean of whiteness.

"Boys!" It was Mr. Gunderson's voice at the foot of the stairs. "Get up! We got cows waitin' to be milked!"

Acorn rolled over and looked at me. "It's storming," I said. "Hear that wind?"

We both scrambled downstairs just as fast as we could go.

The Missus had our oatmeal ready. "No school today," she said. "You boys hang on to the rope to get to the barn."

Acorn shot me a quiet smile. I knew we were both thinking the same thing—more time!

The storm blasted for three days. Twice a day we'd

trudge through the swirling snow to the barn and back, heads down against the gale. We had the cows to milk and feed, and the chickens, too. Jake and Mr. Gunderson chopped through the ice in the water trough to let the cows take a drink. In the house we hauled coal to keep the stove going and helped Mrs. Gunderson with the cooking. Between chores Jake played checkers with Acorn and me and taught us a game with a rubber ball and metal "jacks" shaped like stars.

The third day I woke up feeling that something was wrong. It took me a while before I realized what it was—the wind had quit, and with the snow wrapped around the farm buildings like great fat mufflers, everything was quiet.

"If you take Black with the sleigh you can probably get through," Mr. Gunderson was saying to Jake when we came downstairs. Jake was looking over Mrs. Gunderson's grocery list. She'd said only last night that she had a stack of eggs and cream she needed delivered to town as soon as the storm broke.

Mr. Gunderson turned and looked at us before he filled his coffee mug. "Roads are blocked," he said. "I got a lot of shoveling you boys can do after the milking. Jake's goin' to town for groceries."

I settled down with my oatmeal, glad to think

there was still another day before there'd be talk of Acorn leaving, when I realized my brother hadn't even got himself a bowl. He was watching Mr. Gunderson as if he was still taking in his words, turning them over. Then he cleared his throat to speak.

"Are the trains runnin', sir?" he asked.

I almost dropped my spoon. All of them, even Mrs. Gunderson, turned to stare at Acorn. His courage, or whatever it was made him want to get everything out in the open, was a thing I couldn't help but admire. Still, I wished he hadn't been so forthright—and I saw Mr. Gunderson frown at it, too.

"Nothin's runnin'," he growled, looking like the sight of Acorn put a bad taste in his mouth. "There was any train runnin', I'd have let you know. You lookin' to get a free ride to town, or what?"

"No, sir," Acorn said, shooting a quick look at me. "Just wanted to know."

Mr. Gunderson gave a grunt. "You'll be shoveling today. That's all you *need* to know."

The Missus handed her husband a plate of pancakes and set a bowl of oatmeal on the table, glancing meaningfully at my brother as if to say he ought to sit down and eat instead of asking questions. His boldness worried me. I couldn't see any reason for it except to show he didn't care, that he really was just passing through. It was a bluff, of course. Acorn would give a sight more than he let on to stick around and enjoy Mrs. Gunderson's cooking, if he had half a chance.

I caught Jake studying me, and I spooned in my oatmeal as if I had an appetite. But Acorn's blunt way had taken all the pleasure out of the extra time we'd been given—our last day was coming on fast.

After milking, Acorn and I shoveled paths to every building on the place. Mr. Gunderson hooked a blade onto the plow to clear the driveway and part-way down the road. All the time Jake was gone to town, we stayed busy. Our last job in the afternoon was peeling supper potatoes. "Well," Mrs. Gunderson said when we'd finished, "we'll just put these on the back of the stove and wait for Jake."

Acorn and I got out the checkers and were just starting our second game when we heard Jake's sleigh. We all helped haul in groceries before Mr. Gunderson sat down to hear the news from town and Acorn and I went back to our game.

"Brought you a letter," Jake said, pulling a long white envelope from his inside coat pocket.

"The trains running?" Mr. Gunderson asked.

Jake shook his head. "Blair said this came in the last day before the storm. It's from the orphanage," he added. He didn't look at Acorn or me, just watched his brother frown as he reached for the envelope.

Acorn and I stole a look at each other as Mr. Gunderson opened it and unfolded the single sheet. He read quickly, his brows knotted into a scowl. We all waited, watching him. When he was finished he glanced up, gave a disgusted sigh, and handed the letter to Jake.

"Read it yourself," he said.

Jake studied the words for a moment before he flattened the creases on the table and began:

Dear Mr. and Mrs. Gunderson,

I am writing regretfully to inform you that the younger brother of the Smith boy—who is staying with you on your farm—has run away from the orphanage. We have searched for him in every likely place, expecting he would turn up in a few days, but I have come to suspect the boy may have tried to run off and join his brother. In the unlikely event he should find your place, I am asking that you keep him until I can send someone after him. Please inform me if he does arrive there. I ask that you not send him back alone, as I have reason to believe he will not return here.

Please assure his brother that I will send word

*immediately should we have news from this end. I
hope he will not worry unduly.*

*Respectfully,
Jedediah Blake, Headmaster
St. Paul Orphanage*

A frown furrowed Jake's brow as he set down the
letter and looked up at his brother. Mr. Gunderson
was scowling even deeper, having taken in the words
a second time.

I didn't breathe.

"No mention of *my* letter to *him*," Mr. Gunderson
grumbled, pushing back his chair and standing up.
"All right," he growled at Acorn and me, "get up,
both of you, and give me your attention."

We didn't waste any time scrambling to our feet.
Mr. Gunderson's eyes flicked over Acorn as if he was
an annoying little bug and then settled hard on me. I
knew it didn't please him any having the headmaster
issuing him written orders. "Did you tell your brother
how close you are to going back to that orphanage
yourself?" he snapped.

My throat was so dry I could only manage a nod.

"What did I say it would take to send you right
back there?"

I cleared my throat. "Just one more mistake, sir."

"One more mistake," Mr. Gunderson growled, keeping his stormy gaze set on my face. Then he turned to Acorn. "One more mistake," he said again, watching close to see it sink in. "I got a voucher, see, to use to send your brother back at the end of a year. Blake give it to me. I'm going to write him, tell him to send one for you—tell him I'll send you both back together."

Mr. Gunderson paused and pulled in a deep breath. His eyes fell on the letter again, and his face reddened another shade deeper. He pointed a finger at Acorn. "You run away from *here*, nobody's comin' lookin', you hear me? I'm not in the business of baby-sittin' orphans till some schoolmaster comes after 'em. And if you *stay* here, you work. But I'll tell you one thing—I'm not puttin' up with sass. *One mistake*"—his finger shook as he said it, and his voice shook, too, he was that mad—"and both you and your brother are out of here. Voucher or no voucher, I'll send you back. Do you understand me?"

Acorn nodded, his eyes as round as saucers.

"One mistake," Mr. Gunderson repeated, "from either of you." I didn't look away until he did.

"Both of 'em damned worthless for anything in

the winter," he muttered before he caught his wife's quick frown. He jutted his chin. "Just like the horses," he told her, "useless hay burners all winter long."

My knees felt wobbly. Mr. Blake's letter had bought us more time, I could see that, and it was a relief. Acorn, though, tough and brassy as he was, could send us packing with just a word. And I knew we couldn't count on weather or letters bailing us out again.

Mr. Wolverton's Warning

Mr. Gunderson sent a note to Mr. Wolverton about Acorn starting school. He was scratching out a letter to Mr. Blake at the orphanage when we left in the morning, crossing out sentences and rewriting them, getting more red faced by the minute.

At school Mr. Wolverton eyed the note and Acorn warily. I wondered if he was feeling a little overwhelmed with orphans this term.

He pointed Acorn to a seat with the sixth graders, right next to Leroy Johnson. The two of them acted as if they were already good friends, chatting away like everybody else about all the snow they'd had to shovel and the news of a family who'd gotten lost in the storm and survived only because they'd found a barn with cows to keep them warm and fed with milk. No one asked if Acorn and I were brothers and I didn't see any reason to bring it up—that would only bring more questions. Like why hadn't I said so in the first place? And why hadn't he come here with me in the first place? Mostly I didn't want to have to say how close Acorn and I were to a train ride back.

Generally things seemed to return to normal. Acorn joined in the teams the sixth-grade boys formed on the playground, and I stayed with the eighth graders. He was surprised the first day I went down to clean out the horse barn after school. He watched me work while I explained to him what had happened with Leroy Johnson and Pete and Mike.

"You shouldn't of had to take the same punishment as them," he flashed hotly after I'd told him the story.

I snorted out a little laugh. I'd forgotten how sure Acorn was of his opinions, unlike me, who had to tramp around and look at a thing from all angles before I could make a decision on it.

Acorn studied me a moment longer. That fiery look flared in his eyes, sparking an uneasy feeling inside me. Then, with a sigh, he jumped down from his perch on a stall gate, grabbed a pitchfork, and helped me finish.

Mr. Wolverton was surprised to find us both there when he came to check my work. "This is not a job everyone has to do," he pointed out to Acorn. "It is a punishment several boys brought on themselves."

I held my breath for fear Acorn would lay out the unfairness of the situation. But all Acorn said was, "Yeah, he explained that to me."

"Well, it's kindly of you to help out. You two seem to be a couple of kindred spirits," the schoolmaster observed.

I wondered, did a kindred spirit have to do with being kin?

Acorn knew better. "It means we're . . . a lot alike," he explained. "I think he meant it's a good thing for me to help out another orphan."

That was the thing about Acorn. He'd picked up a lot of information from other boys at the orphanage, with the easy way he made friends. Everything was easy for Acorn—like how quick he gave a name to Lady, as if he knew it just by looking at her. It seemed the puppy already knew it, too, and was just waiting for someone to say it. I started wondering if everything is born with a name and people just have to dig down and get acquainted before it can be uncovered. For people like Acorn it was easy digging, a sort of sixth sense, like Lady's keen sense of smell.

✳ ✳ ✳

At the Gundersons', Acorn did his best to fit in. He had his own way of seeing things, of course, and one of them involved Lady. Jake may have thought the pup would be content to stay out in the barn with the cows, but after Jake mentioned that she had a sister and two brothers back at Al's place, Acorn worried that she was lonely. Twice he woke in the middle of the night and slipped down to the barn to curl up with the little collie. Jake found Acorn in the morning and brought him in to breakfast. The first time it happened Mr. Gunderson paid no attention, but the second time he lost his patience.

"What you keep goin' down to the barn in the middle of the night for?" he stormed.

Acorn bit his lip and glanced up at Jake before he answered. "I heard Lady crying," he said. "She gets lonely out there. She's not used to havin' no family at all."

"It's the dead of winter," Mr. Gunderson growled, glaring at Acorn again. "I got to give you a whippin' to beat some sense into you?"

Mrs. Gunderson stood right behind her husband's chair, still holding the oatmeal spoon in her hand. She pointed it at my brother. "You'll catch your death running out like that in the cold," she warned him. Jake was watching Acorn, too, his eyes thoughtful.

"Catch *his* death . . . " Mr. Gunderson muttered irritably. "Slides the barn door back, prob'ly leaves it half open, chills the whole place down. Next thing we'll have calves with pneumonia."

"Maybe the pup would be happy sleeping in my house," Jake said quietly.

Mr. Gunderson dismissed this suggestion with a snort. "That dog ain't lonely," he informed Acorn squarely. "Even if she was, you couldn't hear her cryin'. It's only your imagination. Anyhow, a dog cries like that is just actin' spoiled. She belongs in the barn and you belong in the house!"

"Jake said—" Acorn pleaded.

"I heard what Jake said," Mr. Gunderson barked. "Jake don't need no spoiled puppy to pick up after!" He snatched his spoon and scooped up a heap of oatmeal mush, clearly closing the case.

Mrs. Gunderson sighed and motioned Acorn to come to the table and eat. I shoveled my breakfast in as fast as I could and grabbed up Acorn's and my school things.

"You got no business arguing with Mr. Gunderson," I warned as we trudged across the snowy field to school. "You're lucky he only thought about a whipping. He's not fooling that he won't take no sass, Acorn."

My brother only shrugged. It was like talking to the dried grasses and brush that poked through the snow. I didn't know how I was going to make Acorn understand he couldn't just do whatever he felt like . . . couldn't pull any of the shenanigans he'd pulled at the orphanage. Mr. Gunderson had made his position clear—one mistake and we were finished.

I tried to think, all through the school day and all through chores that night, what I could say to Acorn that would impress him more than what Mr. Gunderson had already said. Acorn never liked to be told what to do, but he especially didn't like to hear it coming from me.

When he woke up the next morning, my brother had a big grin on his face. "Finally got a good night's sleep," he crowed cheerfully. "Lady didn't cry at all, beddin' down in Jake's house."

"What do you mean?" I asked.

Acorn wiped the smile away, seeing the stormy look on my face. "Jake told me last night," he said. "Told me not to say anything—he'd let Lady bunk under his bed."

I stared at my brother and then had to look away. It gave me an odd feeling knowing Jake had taken up for Acorn like that. In a way it made me glad, but in another way it seemed that I'd been left out of a scheme between the two of them. It was a hard spot I was in and a lot harder now that Acorn had arrived.

The thing was, he didn't seem to care nearly as much as I did about making a place here at the Gundersons'. Maybe that's the advantage of being the youngest— you've always got your big brother to handle the worrying.

＊ ＊ ＊

It was the first week in February when I got in trouble again at school. It all started harmlessly enough, with everyone out in the schoolyard for noon recess. The boys had creamed the girls, as usual, at a game of steal sticks. We boys were prancing around, waving the captured sticks in the air to let everybody know about our victory. Then the girls began to chase us, trying to grab their sticks back.

Helen and a seventh-grade girl named Violet ganged up on me, blocking my escape. Suddenly Helen reached in and started tickling my ribs so Violet could snatch the sticks. I laughed from the tickling but kept up my guard. Then Violet knocked me forward. I was shoved against Helen, who fell backward, clutching at my coat and pulling me down with her. We sprawled on the hard, frozen ground, and Violet fell on top of us.

Helen got her hand on my sticks and gave a jerk, but I jerked back harder and somehow the sharp end of one of the sticks gouged her cheek. She flung a hand to her face, her eyes wide with surprise. When she pulled her hand away and saw it streaked red, she started screaming bloody murder. "Get off me!" she yelled, kicking and pummeling my chest. She yanked my coat, and I heard a rip.

Now *I* was mad. I grabbed her coat and gave a rough shake that popped off a button before I shook myself free and sprang up.

Helen was still yelling as she picked herself up off the ground, keeping one hand pressed to her cheek. "You *hit* me!" she cried. "And you tore my coat!"

I took a few steps back, a cold fear seeping through my veins. Mr. Wolverton had warned the class to keep him informed if Pete or I beat up anyone else.

The other kids had quit their tussling and stopped to stare at Helen's bloody face. I looked down at my sticks, vaguely surprised to find them still in my hand.

"Someone get Mr. Wolverton," one of the girls cried. Violet ran up and put her arm around Helen's shoulders, leading her, wailing, to the schoolhouse.

I looked at the faces around me. Some were wide-eyed with fear, as if I'd slapped on war paint and brandished a bloody hatchet. The boys dropped their sticks then, all of them, in little broken clusters on the ground. I threw mine down, too, though I knew it wouldn't do any good.

In another minute Mr. Wolverton hurried around the corner of the school, his coat and pants flapping loosely as the wind hit him. I saw Acorn elbow his way to the front of the circle of kids, eyeing the teacher, his eyes smoldering as though he were ready for a fight.

"What's going on here?" Mr. Wolverton shouted, pointing a bony finger at me. Some of the boys shuffled their feet, looking at the ground. "What do you mean by attacking Helen?" Mr. Wolverton halted with his beaked nose only inches from my face.

"I . . . we were fighting over the sticks," I managed to stammer.

"Sticks!" the teacher sneered. "Fighting over sticks!" He hurled my words back at me as if they were weapons themselves.

I licked my lips, trying to think what to say. Out of the corner of my eye I saw Acorn take a step closer, clenching his fists.

"We were all doing it," someone declared.

Mr. Wolverton whirled. I glanced over his shoulder, taking a quick breath.

For a moment neither of us could tell who had

spoken; it was as if the words had formed themselves in the cold air. Then Mollie stepped forward, her dark braids flapping below her cap. "We girls were all chasing the boys," she said clearly. "They'd got all the sticks and were celebrating. We were trying to grab them."

"Yeah," a few more voices agreed. I looked around at my schoolmates. Their faces were tight with fear, but they were nodding, standing up for me.

Acorn glanced around quickly at the others, too.

"No one else is bleeding," Mr. Wolverton countered, his eyes sweeping the circle of faces. "You other boys must not have lost *your* tempers fighting back."

I bit my lip.

"Violet pushed him down," Mollie said, her voice as clear as the school bell. "He fell on Helen and she started fighting him."

Mr. Wolverton turned back to me and he spotted the tear in my coat at about the same instant I remembered it was there.

"You cut her with the stick?" he questioned, his voice quiet now.

"It was an accident," I said, breathing in courage from Mollie.

He glanced again at my torn coat. Then he swung

his gaze around the circle. "Does anyone else have more to say?" he demanded.

"You could . . . you could go ask Violet. She was the closest," one girl suggested. Others nodded.

"Yes, I shall question Violet," Mr. Wolverton agreed, still scanning their faces. "And anyone who saw more, but has not come forward, may speak to me at my desk. Meanwhile, let's all go in and get back to our lessons."

I took a lungful of cool, freeing air and marched in with the rest.

Mr. Wolverton waited at the door. He motioned for me to stand to the side until the others had gone in, then took a step toward me before he spoke. "I don't know how you get yourself in so much trouble," he said, his eyes very stern, but perhaps not unkind. "Just take this as a word to the wise: You've got to watch your step more than the others. You've got to know your place. You're not like them. You're an orphan. You can be sent right back where you came from, in the blink of an eye. You can't afford to be pulled into fights."

He kept his eyes on my face a minute longer before he turned abruptly and strode into the schoolroom.

My chest felt tight. Mr. Wolverton was warning me: I wasn't to forget who I was; he wouldn't forget, either. Even though he had seemed to believe Mollie and the others, he'd made it clear I still had no place here—no claim to belonging—like the others had. For some reason it brought back what Mrs. Gunderson had said about Gus being a disappointment, but still and all, a son. I began to see there was something all of them knew that I had never understood. I still didn't understand it, but I could feel it, all right. It had a lot to do with having a place. And being *sure* of that place, no matter what.

I heard a sound and whirled to see Acorn straggling up to the door, the last to arrive. I hoped he hadn't heard Mr. Wolverton. I hoped he felt the way I had only those few minutes before, with Mollie and the others sticking up for me. As if in that brief moment I'd *had* a rightful place—and the kids at Hawkeye School had seen me as more than just a plain, gray orphan boy.

Acorn Makes Plans

The new calves started arriving in April. Acorn took to running down to the barn first thing every morning to see if any had come. And it was the last thing he did at night, slipping out from the privy just to peek into the barn before he came to bed. We had to teach the calves how to drink from a pail so they wouldn't be stealing all their mother's milk as they grew older. At first they snorted and backed away when their noses touched the liquid, but Jake showed us how to put our fingers into the calves' mouths to make them suck. Then we gradually lowered our hands into the pail so they'd *have* to slurp up some milk as they sucked our fingers. Pretty soon they were drinking. Acorn couldn't keep from giggling every time he felt their rough tongues straining to suck, tickling his skin. I think he missed it when they didn't need him anymore. He always wanted to watch them even when they got older and no one had to hold the pail.

"You best take good care of those calves," Mr. Gunderson told us one night. "That's how a fellow learns to take care of his own, paying attention to things when he's young."

"How does a fellow get himself a calf?" Acorn put in right away.

Mr. Gunderson sized up my brother. "Hard work, boy. Everything I got, I got by hard work."

Acorn looked down at Bessie's little red-and-white calf and rubbed her coarse hair. I could see he was turning Mr. Gunderson's words over in his mind. "I *will* work hard for you, Mr. Gunderson," he solemnly declared.

Maybe my brother had already forgotten what Mr. Gunderson had told us the day he got a letter back from Mr. Blake with a train voucher inside for Acorn. "Going to hold on to this," he'd said. "Kept you all winter doin' nothing, might as well keep you on to get some work out of you, long as you don't give me trouble." He hadn't changed his mind a bit about sending me right back when my year was up.

Now Mr. Gunderson shot Acorn a look of cool distaste. "And I'll be watching you," he grumped before he straightened and moved on to the next calf.

Right away I saw Acorn's quick, pleased grin. He hadn't seen Mr. Gunderson's look, and I thought that was a good thing as I watched my brother give Bessie's heifer a final pat, a dreamy look lighting his eyes. He turned and caught me watching him, and he grinned again. "Going to name her Sunny," he told me.

I should have known right then Acorn didn't understand anything at all about Mr. Gunderson.

✳ ✳ ✳

"You think the Gundersons are maybe deciding to adopt us?" Acorn asked later that night as we were getting undressed for bed.

I turned from slinging my overalls on the peg to stare at him. "No, Acorn," I said flat out.

"He said he'd be watchin' my work with the calves."

"He watches everything on his farm. That doesn't change the fact that he's going to send us back." I didn't bother to inform my brother that Mr. Gunderson would only be watching him to make sure he wasn't making mistakes.

"Well, I ain't going back," Acorn declared solemnly. "And you ain't, neither."

I jumped in under the bedcovers and turned to stare up at him in the light of the bare bulb that hung from the ceiling. "Can't very well refuse to go," I told him.

" 'Course not!" Acorn glanced at the floor grate and lowered his voice. "That's why we've got to plan. I'm startin' a little pile of supplies for us to take when we run away."

I gaped at him. "Where are you going to run to, Acorn?"

"Hop a freight," Acorn answered, as if it were too obvious to need saying. "Just find an empty boxcar. Open door is what to watch for. You go east, you see, to Chicago." Acorn plopped down next to me on the bed, his eyes shining. "Then you hop off and find a train headin' south. It's warm in the south. No winter. No snow. Just hitch a ride down there and get a job pickin' oranges or peaches or something. When you're done in one place, you hop back on a freight and go somewhere else. Easy as pie."

"What supplies are you piling up?" I asked him, suspiciously.

"Canned things," he said. "And flour and salt. Coffee. I found where Mrs. Gunderson keeps her empty canning jars and I helped myself to a few. I can slip a little of this and that in every now and then and pretty soon we'll have everything we need."

"That's stealing!" I burst out.

"It's only extra I could be eating if I wanted to," Acorn shot back smoothly. "I'm just choosing to save it up instead of eating it all."

I knew he wasn't being entirely honest. Flour wasn't something you helped yourself to; it came baked in things. And we didn't often drink coffee; mostly it was for the grown-ups. Still, he had a point. There did seem to be plenty.

"Where're you keeping your supply?" I asked.

Acorn grinned. "Right under their noses. No, I mean, right *over* their noses. I found those jars in the little room at the head of the stairs. There's a storage trunk in there. Nothin' in it but blankets and pictures. I put my stuff in the bottom, under the blankets, where no one will ever think to look." He stretched full length on the bed. "There's more stuff I found in the other two rooms." Even though his voice was hushed, I could tell he was really proud of his scavenging. "And more out in the farthest granary. There's no grain in it, just old tools and things."

I was dumbstruck. What would the Gundersons think if they knew what Acorn was doing?

But what really bothered me was that my brother was so cheerfully confident that we could live off the land, carelessly swiping a few things here and there, just as he was doing with the Gundersons. Acorn didn't care about making a place on this farm. I had thought, watching him earlier with the calves, that he was beginning to settle into wanting what I wanted. Now I could see he was only biding his time until the right moment came to escape to a bigger and grander adventure than ever. Only this time I would be swept along with him—swept farther and farther away from everything I hoped for.

✳ ✳ ✳

It was easy enough, I discovered after Acorn let me in on his plan, to find times to explore the other up-stairs rooms. Everything Acorn told me was true. The rooms were used for storage, even the bedroom next to ours, which had a bed and dresser all set out as if Mrs. Gunderson were expecting company. The closet of that next-door room contained the item that fascinated Acorn the most—a dusty old army rifle.

"We could use this out on the land," he breathed, running his fingers over its long, smooth barrel.

"We ain't stealing any gun," I stated firmly.

He didn't seem to hear. "I even found where Gunderson keeps his bullets." He glanced at the top shelf of the closet.

"Acorn," I argued desperately, "you don't even know how to load a gun."

That got his attention. Acorn glared at me, his eyes narrowed slits. "Maybe *you* don't know how to load a gun," he corrected me, "but I do."

I knew he wasn't bluffing.

Especially later when he showed me the things he'd hoarded. He held up the jars one by one. He'd saved all kinds of stuff. I couldn't believe my eyes.

"How come you got two flours?" I asked.

"One's baking powder."

I held a mustard-colored powder to the light.

"I think that's ginger," he said. "And this brown one is cloves."

If he hadn't looked so serious, I'd have laughed. "You'll need to steal a whole library of cookbooks to use all this stuff. Where are you going to be baking cookies? Over the open fire?"

Acorn squirmed. "I thought a little spice would liven things up."

"What's this?" I asked, holding up another jar.

"Rat poison." Then, in answer to my startled look, "You can't trust everybody, you know."

Goose bumps budded on my arms. The powder was the same black-brown color as the coffee and cloves. "You have to label these things, Acorn. Rat-poison coffee could kill *us*, you know. Besides, what if Lady got into it?"

"I hadn't thought of that," he admitted, a little deflated. But not for long. "Do you really think we can take Lady with us?" he asked.

I studied him, taking a slow breath to consider how to tell him the truth. "Acorn," I said carefully, "this plan won't work. Besides, it ain't the end of the world if the Gundersons send us back. We can work at the orphanage till we get us a real job somewhere."

"*You* don't have to worry," he shot back, snatching the rat poison out of my hands and stuffing it back into the trunk with the other jars. "You're finishing eighth grade. *You* might get a job—I'll have to stay in school. They'll *never* let me out of that orphanage!"

I sighed. It was hopeless arguing with Acorn. "Look," I said, making my voice as firm as I could, "we can't steal stuff from the Gundersons. They've been good to us. Think how they'd feel if they woke up one morning with their rifle and everything gone. They'd never think the same of us!"

Acorn eyed me coldly. "Why should I care what they think of us when we're never going to see 'em again?"

His words scared me. But what scared me worse was the sudden thought that maybe Acorn's ideas made more sense than mine did. All this time, I'd kept on hoping somehow I could change Mr. Gunderson's mind and make him want me. It was all I worked for, all I worried over, all that kept me looking ahead. What if I was just fooling myself?

Later, thinking about it long after everyone else was sound asleep and a fox was yipping somewhere in the night, I realized how different Acorn and I looked at things. Even if I had a paid ticket to the other end of the world, I could never let Jake down by running off without telling him. I could never steal the Gundersons' things.

But I also knew that when the time came and Acorn refused to be sent back to the orphanage, I couldn't let him run off without me. He didn't see things the way I did, but still he was my brother.

Avenging Old Wrongs

Acorn did manage to stay clear of trouble at school. Mr. Wolverton seemed to like him, letting him clean erasers with Leroy when they were done early with their work. Sometimes I heard Acorn answer a question real sharp and quick, and I would look up to see a smile of approval on the teacher's face.

It was the other kids who acted up more and more as spring melted the snow and pushed new green grass shoots up out of the softening earth.

A note appeared on Helen's desk one day, signed with Mike Mobridge's initials. It read: *"Dearest Helen, I wish I could give you a big kiss on the lips! M.M."*

Helen showed the note to Violet Martin, and in no time everyone in school knew what it said. "I never wrote that!" Mike declared, shaking his head and backing away when the girls showed it to him on the playground.

"Well, we have proof," Violet declared. "Nobody else in school has those initials!" Helen tossed her yellow hair and narrowed her eyes at Mike, warning him to keep his distance. It surprised me that Mike was daring enough to write the note, for he was blushing red as a beet, not even looking at Helen, much less acting inclined to kiss her.

Another day a tack appeared on Mr. Wolverton's chair. Actually there may have been three or four. He sat down and shot right up, howling. We all nearly choked trying not to laugh.

Everyone looked around, trying to locate the culprit. Mr. Wolverton marched immediately to the back of the room and ordered us older students to open our desks for inspection. "Stand and turn your pockets inside out!" he commanded.

I saw Pete's scowl change to a look of shock and surprise as a little box of tacks skimmed out across the aisle when he kicked back his chair to stand up. I knew what it was as soon as Mr. Wolverton swooped and snatched it off the floor—I'd seen a box just like it in Mrs. Gunderson's "junk" drawer in the kitchen.

A gasp went up from every corner of the room. I

thought I heard Pete suck in his breath, too. He seemed as surprised as the rest of us.

"How do you explain this, Pete Morrison?" the teacher demanded.

"I dunno. I dunno," Pete repeated, shaking his head.

Most of the class seemed to believe Pete was guilty and was simply doing a fine job of acting. But I wasn't so sure.

Pete received ten sharp raps on the backside from Mr. Wolverton's willow switch. The schoolmaster drew his arm back for a full swing and put so much muscle into delivering each blow that sweat popped out on his brow. Everyone in the room was quiet. I couldn't even hear feet wiggling. Acorn turned around to glance at me with a lively gleam in his eye.

But the strangest incident of all happened during our spring cleanup. It was the next-to-the-last day of school, the sky feathery with wispy clouds, the air soft, the sun warm, though the breeze was crisp. Mr. Wolverton had some of the older boys bring ladders so they could putty the windowpanes while the girls washed the windows and cleaned the chalkboards. Other students swept the classroom floor, polished the desks, and scrubbed down the steps. It was my day to clean the horse barn, so Mr. Wolverton sent me down early while the others finished the playground cleaning. I was happy to think I could be done ahead of the usual time.

The first I knew of all the commotion was when I heard running footsteps and looked up to see Acorn hurl himself through the doorway. He snatched up the extra pitchfork and set to work at a fever pace.

"I'm almost done," I called out, but Acorn didn't seem to hear. He began whistling a little tune. Every now and then he'd stop, and his shoulders would twitch as if he were laughing.

It wasn't long until I heard the schoolmaster's quick, solid steps approaching the barn. Acorn whirled and stepped over close to me. "Remember, I been here helpin' you the whole time," he said.

I frowned, not understanding what he meant.

"Ah, here you are!" Mr. Wolverton exclaimed, spotting Acorn as he stepped into the dim barn. "Have you been here working all along?"

" 'Course I have," Acorn replied. "Just ask *him* if I been helpin'."

I wished I could burrow right down under the straw. I hated lying, even for my own brother.

Mr. Wolverton hardly glanced my way. "Come with me," he said to Acorn. "We've a bit of a problem."

The schoolmaster's voice sounded tight with anger, but I didn't think it was directed at my brother.

I followed them into the sunlight and up the hill. It took me a few minutes to notice the outhouse lying on its side, the boys' door thrown open at a crazy angle.

There was a cluster of boys and girls standing a little way off, the girls holding their noses, the boys yelling back and forth. Pete and Leroy stood facing each other, away from the others. Pete's fists clenched and unclenched as he glared at Leroy, his knees crouched and ready to lunge. The younger boy stood poised like a rabbit with his toes dug in, set to spring away.

The rest of the kids gathered around as Mr. Wolverton strode up the hill.

Leroy Johnson smiled a little when he saw Acorn. The two of them had become good friends.

"All right," Mr. Wolverton barked. "All concerned parties are present. Let us begin again. First I want to know if anyone saw who locked the outhouse door."

"I locked it, Mr. Wolverton," Leroy Johnson confessed, straightening. "I thought it was empty."

"Thought it was empty?" Pete bellowed, taking a step toward him.

Mr. Wolverton put up a warning hand.

"Did you check to see if the door was locked from the inside?" Mr. Wolverton asked Leroy without turning his head from Pete.

"No," Leroy admitted after a second's hesitation.

Everyone started yelling at once.

Mr. Wolverton held up both hands for silence, glaring around the ring of us.

"Tell him, Acorn," Leroy demanded, "tell him what you told me—that Mr. Wolverton said it was our job to move the outhouse to a new hole."

My heart bumped heavily against my ribs. That was an old trick some of the boys had tried at the orphanage a few times. Get some new kid to tip the outhouse when there was no fresh hole dug.

"Said I told him *what?*" Mr. Wolverton repeated.

"No," Acorn said, shaking his head. "I never said anything like that, Mr. Wolverton."

I glanced at Leroy. He was staring at Acorn in stunned disbelief. It occurred to me then that he had asked Mr. Wolverton to go to the barn to find Acorn. Clearly he expected my brother to be an ally.

My stomach started churning.

"How am I to know the truth?" Mr. Wolverton challenged Leroy coldly. "Are you trying to get *this* boy in trouble?"

It hit me that the teacher was taking Acorn's side, reminding Leroy he'd been quick to get one orphan in trouble that first time. But something else was also suddenly shiny clear—Acorn must have cleverly planned the whole thing! He knew Leroy had misled the schoolmaster once, so Mr. Wolverton would be wary of being misled by him again. To all the others it looked as though Leroy had tipped the outhouse to pay Pete back and was trying to save his own hide by pointing the finger at Acorn. Only Acorn and I knew the truth.

Pete shook his fist at Leroy. A picture of him lashing the rope around the younger boy's chest flashed into my mind. I saw him jabbing the gelding with the willow stick and I heard him hiss, "You don't breathe a word to anyone about this," straight into Leroy's terrified face.

"Wait, Mr. Wolverton," I said, stepping forward. "I think . . . I think I can explain what happened here." I took a couple of deep breaths to stop my voice from shaking. I looked Mr. Wolverton square in the eye.

"It's something I said to him last night," I said, jerking my head toward Acorn. "We were doing chores, at home. I mentioned that in the spring people usually dig a new outhouse hole. Told him I thought that we might have to do that today."

Acorn was watching me, his face growing pale. "He must have misunderstood, thought I said the hole was already dug. He must have figured the outhouse would have to be moved today and said something like that to Leroy." I babbled on, making up the story as fast as my mind could crank it out. "As soon as he heard the thumping from inside the outhouse, I think my brother got scared and came running to the barn to check with me to see if I hadn't told him the schoolmaster said to move it. I just came up here to try to straighten out the misunderstanding." I could hardly recognize my own voice, I was talking so smooth and so slick.

Pete squinted skeptically at me. Twenty-some other faces stared at me, too, their jaws agape in surprise. Leroy's eyes were fastened on mine, relief dawning on his face.

But Acorn's eyes were slits, as if he'd drawn a curtain between us.

"Your brother?" Mollie said as if she'd never heard the words before.

"Yeah," I said, feeling a ripple of relief. I nodded quickly, even daring to grin a little at the teacher.

He hesitated an instant and then smiled back at me. "You behaved very maturely here today," he said, "speaking up and telling the truth. That is commendable. Done like a gentleman!" His eyes were warm, I thought, even friendly.

"All right!" Mr. Wolverton turned around to the others, snapping back to the business at hand. "Let's all push together and get this outhouse set back in place. No harm's been done. It was all a misunderstanding and no one's been hurt."

The others exploded like a dam breaking, all laughing and joking and making wisecracks. I took ahold of the edge of the outhouse and began to push, glancing around to see where Acorn had gone. He wasn't anywhere in sight.

Leroy Johnson's eyes met mine as if he'd been studying me for a while. Staring back at him, a lot of things suddenly came clear. Acorn had set Leroy up to face the wrath of Pete. Surely he had also been the one who laid the tacks on the teacher's chair and put the box behind Pete's place at the back table. He'd probably written the note to Helen and signed Mike's initials, too. He'd paid them all back, all those who had tricked me or lied about me to Mr. Wolverton after that day in the horse barn. It was Acorn's idea of what brothers were for.

I choked down the acid taste in my throat, wondering what Acorn was thinking about me now, after the dumb lie I'd concocted. I'd told the whole school that my brother had run scared to me, when the truth was Acorn possessed not a morsel of fear. What else could I have said? I knew Acorn would never understand why I'd taken Leroy's part. And why had I? I guess because I had wronged Leroy. I was the one who'd talked so fast and so sneaky to lure him to the barn. My clever tongue had gotten me in trouble that time, too.

As I trudged home later, I thought about how Mr. Wolverton had believed Acorn so readily in the barn. Acorn had a way of softening people. It had taken me months to win the teacher's approval—and he really only gave it when he thought Acorn was being set up and he'd started to see maybe he'd judged us both wrong.

But it didn't matter anymore what Mr. Wolverton thought of me, or what any of them at school thought of me. The real test would come when I got home and faced Acorn. I knew I wouldn't have one single smooth word left to say.

Armed and Dangerous

Jake and Acorn were hitching up Babe and Black to a flat wooden sled they called a stone boat when I went down to the barn. "Hello," Jake hollered. Acorn didn't even cut me a glance. "Find all the rocks you can," Jake shouted after us as we headed for the field. I gave him a wave. Acorn didn't look back. He just flicked the reins as if he were in a hurry.

When we got to the field, Acorn dropped the reins and right away started picking up rocks. Babe and Black stood waiting patiently.

"Acorn," I said, following after him and grabbing his arm to make him look at me, "we've got to talk."

Acorn pulled away. He had three fist-sized stones cradled in one arm, and he stooped to pick up another one as he turned back to the boat.

"Look," I persisted, "I know you were getting those guys because of what they did to me, but that's all in the past. They don't bother me and I don't bother them."

Acorn dumped his load and started grabbing up rocks as fast as he could and firing them at the boat.

"I'm sorry for making up the story about you running to me, Acorn," I said, pleading with him. "But I didn't want to see Pete have another excuse to beat up Leroy, and I couldn't think of any other way to get everybody out of trouble."

Acorn shot a look at me then. "Leroy done you in once," he snapped. "I took your side. You work so hard saving *his* hide, but me you call a coward."

"I didn't—"

"Said I was scared! It's the same thing," he shouted, hurling another rock at the boat and facing me square.

"I never meant to take you down, Acorn, I only—"

"You ain't really no brother of mine," Acorn hollered as if he couldn't bear even the sound of my voice anymore. "You wouldn't say that thing about me—"

"You never told me what you were planning!" I spewed out before I even thought. "You could have talked to me about it; we could have figured it out together. Instead you came running down to the barn right in front of Mr. Wolverton expecting me to lie for you. I don't like lying, Acorn!"

"You didn't mind lyin' for Leroy!"

He had me cold. I stared at him, swallowing hard and fighting that sick feeling in my gut. I wasn't ready for what he said next.

"Where's my knife?" His voice was low and quiet.

My stomach clenched up like a hard fist. "I have it," I said, trying to keep my voice easy. "I kept it like I told you." I didn't know what Acorn had in mind to do with that knife, but I knew it was nothing good.

"Give it to me," he said.

"It's put away. At the house. What do you want it for?"

"I want to keep it myself."

I stared at him, hearing what he hadn't said. That he couldn't trust me with his prize possession anymore.

Before I could say anything else, he grabbed a rock, then slammed it hard onto the stone boat and whirled to face me again. He doubled his fists. "You never would have sent for me, would you?" His voice was heavy and flat as a chunk of lead hitting water.

He looked at me, then away, stuffing his fists in his pockets. "You don't know what it was like back at the orphanage. It was harder, way worse, because every-body knew my brother had pulled out. But I remem-bered what you'd done for me, hiding the knife. I believed you'd come back, any day. *Any day*."

I slowly shook my head, wanting to stop the gush of his words and thinking he'd probably hit me if I said the wrong thing. I wasn't afraid to fight him, but I *was* scared that whatever I said would only make it worse.

"I try to show you I'm a good brother," he blurted, flinging an arm out as he talked. "I help you muck out the school barn. I think up ways to get even with Pete and Leroy. And you . . ." Acorn paused and took a breath, blinking rapidly. "You won't even tell 'em we're *brothers*, not till it's like you're apologizing for knowing me. You say I'm a coward! And me"—Acorn stabbed a finger at his own heaving chest—"*me* you say you won't lie for! Not for *me!*"

He didn't wait for my answer. He turned and ran in a blind, stumbling gait across the field to the thicket of willows at the bottom of the draw.

"Acorn! Wait!" I shouted. Babe and Black turned and cocked their ears toward me, as though even they knew I was wasting my voice. I was sick and ashamed, suddenly seeing all the times Acorn had felt I'd be-trayed him.

"Wait!" I shouted again. I wanted to run after Acorn and tell him all the new things I felt—to grab him and make him listen to me—but I had to stay with the horses, I couldn't leave them. All I could do was wave my arms like a fool and shout Acorn's name.

I tried to pick a few rocks, but I couldn't concentrate on the job. I kept watching the draw, hoping Acorn would reappear. He was mad at me, but he wouldn't leave for good without all his supplies, that's what I told myself.

Finally, when I heard Jake calling the cows, I had to give up and drive Babe and Black over to the rock pile to unload.

✳ ✳ ✳

It was a relief when Acorn appeared at milking time. He wouldn't even look at me, though, and I could see that his eyes were swollen and red and two ragged streaks trailed down each cheek through the dirt. Later, when the two of us undressed for bed, I knew I had to try to tell him how wrong he'd read me and how I planned to change my ways. But he cut me off as soon as I spoke his name.

"I ain't goin' to school tomorrow," he said flatly.

I tried to look him straight in the eye. "I *did* plan to send for you like I promised," I said. "I just needed more time. Acorn, please don't run away. We can still think of a plan before the year is up—"

"I want my knife," he said. "You got no right to keep my things."

I didn't know what to do. Lady, who slipped in and out of the house as easily as any of us now that Mr. Gunderson had gotten used to her, gave a thump of her tail and a whine as she looked from Acorn to me and back. I didn't want to give the knife back. What did he plan to do with it? But he wasn't about to back down. Maybe just having it again would make him feel better. Maybe my giving it to him would be proof that I hadn't ever meant to betray him.

I turned and walked slowly to the closet. I bent down to dig in my bag for the knife. It was even heavier than I remembered. Solid. The hobo who had carved the handle had made himself a good weapon.

I brought it over and held it out to him. "I'm sorry I said what I did about you, Acorn," I told him hoarsely, wrapping my fingers tight around his fist as he grasped the knife. "I was wrong. I *am* proud to be your brother, no matter how it looks. Please, Acorn, I need you to promise me you won't run away tomorrow if I go to school and tell Mr. Wolverton you took sick. You just hide out down in the willows if you want and Mr. Gunderson won't even know. Will you promise me that much?"

I waited, watching him think it over. He pulled away from me, looking down at the knife, running his fingers over the carvings and then turning the blade up and testing it with his thumb.

"I won't run tomorrow," he muttered thickly just when I thought I'd have to grab ahold of him and make him answer me. "I'll hide out, like you said."

I let my breath out easy. "I'll count on that," I told him.

Turning his back to me, he walked over to his side of the bed. After a moment he slid the knife under his pillow and flopped the covers over his head, curling his body under them, and slipping one hand beneath the pillow.

He'd never answered me about his plans for that knife, and I knew he wouldn't tell me now if I asked him. It was one more worry for me, added to a whole heap of worries about what my brother was planning next.

✳ ✳ ✳

In the morning Acorn left the house when I did but stayed in the willow thicket while I went on to school. I felt sure he wouldn't run away without me—he wouldn't want to risk sneaking back into the house to get his supplies.

It was hard to concentrate on long-division races at the blackboard when the whole time I was wondering what Acorn was doing. Not surprisingly, I was the first one out in the spell down.

Mr. Wolverton made a fine speech near the end of the day. "We've had an eventful year," he said, smiling tightly. I thought he looked as pleased as any of us to see the school year end, but grimly pleased, as if he couldn't allow himself to relax until the day came to an end. "I want to congratulate the eighth graders for their fine accomplishments," he went on, letting his eyes rove over us. "You have all passed your eighth-grade examinations, and I have certificates for each of you." His eyes stopped on me. "I urge you all to continue your education. You will never regret attaining more knowledge. Find a way to go on to high school if you can—it will make your life richer forever."

His words had a flourish to them. I could almost see them, glimmering like frozen vapor in the air. His eyes held mine for one last moment, as if he wanted to make sure I grasped the importance of what he said.

Helen passed out candy she called truffles, tied with a bow. "In town school," she informed us, "they have an eighth-grade graduation ceremony and everyone gets presents." She handed me mine with a wide smile that made my heart turn over so fast I wondered for a second if it had stopped for good.

Mr. Wolverton gave us an extra recess in the afternoon. The younger children ran out, shrieking as usual, but we eighth graders strolled out slowly. Maybe everyone was contemplating the teacher's words the same way I was.

"You going to high school, then?" I heard Pete ask Mollie.

She nodded, lowering her eyes.

"I might," he said, even though she hadn't asked him. "I might show up after harvest."

No one asked where I would be next year. Maybe everyone knew orphans only came out for a year at a time. Maybe no one cared.

"Where's your brother?" Mollie asked me quietly when all the others had shuffled off in little groups.

"Took sick," I said, not looking at her.

"I never . . . I never knew he was your brother," she said, stumbling a little on her words, which wasn't like Mollie. "Are you—did you have a family . . . before?"

I bit my lip, wishing I could dodge her questions. "No," I said gruffly. "No, we never had no family."

She stepped back a little, a look of hurt or confusion flitting through her clear brown eyes. "I guess that explains why you're so serious," she said. "You've got to be the one in charge all by yourself."

Someone shouted, and we both turned to look. Mollie ran off to where Helen and the seventh-grade girls were beckoning, and I sauntered over toward the boys by the tree row. I was glad not to have to think how to reply to what she'd said. Mollie was right. I *was* serious. I had to be. Who wouldn't be plumb gloomy thinking they had charge of Acorn?

Today I was more than gloomy—jittery would be closer to the right word. My stomach churned every time I thought of the knife. Dangerous, that was the word for Acorn. Armed and dangerous. Mollie didn't know the half of what being in charge of Acorn could mean.

Dry Tinder, Laid Ready

Mrs. Gunderson was determined that we get the barn painted before haying began. Jake built us a scaffold so that we could walk back and forth painting each board. He put a ladder up from the scaffolding, to reach the peak at the front and back of the barn. Those parts Jake did himself. The rest, the long miles of red, were for Acorn and me.

Acorn seemed to enjoy the back and forth motion of it. He liked to have races to see who could do a board faster, and he liked to set goals of how far we could paint by dinner and then how far before supper. We hadn't talked any more about how mad he'd been at me. Neither of us mentioned the knife. Acorn sometimes chattered on and on about things people had told him of trains, or what he'd read about cattle ranching. At other times he fell coldly silent, slapping up a fence that kept me shut out of what he was thinking. I didn't have the courage to break through that silence by asking questions—I was pretty sure I didn't want to hear the answers anyway.

There were only two times my brother seemed to be his old bright-eyed self—when he was quietly fiddling with his knife, tossing it overhand and then underhand into a tree stump and then testing the blade before he slipped it back inside his shirt again, and when we fed the calves. He'd pat Sunny while he watched her drink, rubbing her neck and murmuring things to her. He even talked Jake into finding him a rope to loop around the calf's neck so he could lead her. But she planted her feet and refused to be led until Jake showed Acorn the trick of carrying oats in his hand and letting her nose it. Times like that, watching the carefree grin on Acorn's face, I let myself hope he'd gotten over his injured feelings and even forgiven me.

But there was no free time for practicing his knife skills or playing with calves while we were painting the barn. About the middle of the third day, even Acorn's chatter had died out completely. The only sound was the slap-slap of our wide brushes on the dry boards.

"Been thinkin' about our problem," Acorn declared out of the blue. His words got my attention.

"What problem?"

He glanced around. " 'Bout you and me." He lowered his voice even though there wasn't anyone nearby. Mrs. Gunderson was baking bread, Jake was finishing the seeding, and Mr. Gunderson had taken cream and eggs to town. "I been thinkin' about how you said it wouldn't work to run away."

I let out a breath of relief. "Yeah?" I prodded, running my brush under the edge of the board.

"I'm thinkin' the main problem is we don't have any money."

"And I suppose next you're going to say you have a plan for striking it rich," I suggested dryly.

"Mrs. G has a teapot full of money."

I glanced at him. "So?"

"So we take some," he said, as casually as if he'd suggested taking cookies on a picnic.

"*Steal* some, you mean," I snapped.

"Mr. G owes me for my calf!" Acorn argued, slapping his paintbrush against the board.

"What calf?"

"The one he said I could earn by working hard for it."

"Acorn, he didn't mean—"

"And I *have* been working hard."

"That's not what he meant, Acorn. He wasn't promising you—"

"He owes me for workin'. And if I'm leavin' the calf here, I got a right to take what I earned!"

"That would be plain robbery," I shot back.

Acorn glared at me, breathing hard. "You call *me* a robber! Mr. G don't even have to pay for somethin' he promised?"

I could see Acorn was fighting tears. Still, I didn't waste time feeling sorry for him; I was too busy trying to figure out how to make him understand. Mollie's words mocked me: "You've got to be the one in charge all by yourself." I wished I could shake Acorn so hard it would knock his way of thinking clean the other direction, like a blast of wind reversing a weather vane.

Instead I tried to make him listen to reason. "You think it would be so great living out on the land. There's no hope for us making it the way you say, Acorn. Nobody'd take us in. We'd have to turn to robbing folks. I'm not a grown man somebody'd hire. I'm only a kid—only two years older than you!"

Acorn answered me with one weary sigh. "Why don't you just ask Jake? He'll tell you I heard right."

I frowned, giving my head a confused little shake. "He'll tell you Mr. Gunderson said I could have a calf of my own."

I could see I was wasting my time. I picked up my brush and dipped it purposefully in the thick red paint. I spread it in a wide stroke, not looking at my brother as I set my jaw and gave him one last piece of advice. "Ask Jake yourself," I told him, "but not when Mr. Gunderson's listening."

Maybe Jake could make Acorn see he was wrong, way wrong, about Mr. Gunderson and the calf. And about what the law would do to two thieving kids living on their own. Maybe Jake could make my brother see how off base he was in his thinking—and even in his hearing—when it came to Mr. Gunderson.

Maybe Jake could head off whatever it was my brother was dreaming up next.

✳ ✳ ✳

As far as I knew, Acorn never asked Jake the question. My answers pushed him back into his cold silence again. It took us another week to finish painting the barn, but we did it without much discussion except pointing out spots the other one missed.

After that came haying, a busy time when even Acorn was too tired at the end of each day to scheme any more. He fell asleep most nights with his clothes on, before I'd even crawled into bed. It was near the end of July, the last of the hay put up in the barn loft, that one night at supper Mr. Gunderson announced we were going to the county fair.

"After milking in the morning, you boys come in and help the Missus get our lunch packed," Mr. Gunderson ordered. "Then we can all go off to town. Jake, you comin' along?"

We all turned to look at Jake. He lifted his head from cutting off a piece of meat and glanced around at our waiting faces. "I might. I guess I might," he said.

"Good." Mr. Gunderson seemed pleased. "I'm guessing we could all fit in the flivver. Now's the time for you to drive it," he said to Jake.

Acorn busted out in an excited grin. I had to smile, too.

"More backseat drivers than I need giving me advice," Jake said, but I could tell he wasn't grumbling for real.

"We won't say a word," Acorn promised with mock sincerity.

Everyone laughed. A warm glow spread through me. I looked over at Acorn's beaming face and I was sure he felt it, too. Maybe . . . maybe there was still some way we could all be a family.

The next morning was bright and sunny. Mr. Gunderson showed Acorn and me how to crank the flivver while Jake sat proudly at the wheel. The engine sputtered and then caught, and we dashed around to find our seats. Mr. Gunderson sat up in front with Jake, and Acorn and I piled in the back with Mrs. Gunderson, who was holding a lunch basket on her lap and a wire egg crate on top of that.

"Push this pedal to start," began Mr. Gunderson, pointing to one of the three pedals on the floor. "That's low gear, forward. The far one is reverse and this one's the brake." Soon we were lurching down the driveway.

It didn't take Jake long to get the feel of driving, and we sailed along in high gear. He didn't drive as fast as Mr. Gunderson, but I didn't mind. Every time Jake turned his head to scan to the right and the left, I could see his ear-to-ear grin and it made my heart glad.

A bank of clouds was forming low in the west. Maybe it would rain and settle the dust. Even rain had to be a good sign, because nothing could ruin a day like this.

We passed the same old barn we'd seen the summer before, when I first arrived in Crosby. It looked more forlorn than ever with that big hole torn out of the roof. "Thought you said someone was movin' that barn," Mr. Gunderson remarked to Jake.

Jake shrugged. "It's what I heard," he said.

"Sure too bad to see it just falling apart." Mr. Gunderson turned his lean shoulder to glance back at it as we swept past. "Wood's all drying up."

Acorn was studying the barn from his seat next to me. "Just take one match," he murmured dreamily, "the whole thing would go up in a flash." His words lit in my mind like a warning flare.

"Be like lighting dry tinder, all right," Mr. Gunderson agreed.

We had to stop to deliver eggs and cream, but at last we chugged over to the fairgrounds. Jake parked the flivver next to a tree, and we all piled out. Mrs. Gunderson tucked the lunch basket down in the shade between the seats before we headed for the exhibits.

We sauntered past rows of cows and calves and chickens in pens. There were hogs in wooden crates, a few sheep, even a goat.

"We should of brought our calves," Acorn muttered.

"Yes, we should have," Mr. Gunderson agreed. "Would have taken first place by the looks of what's here." He spotted a neighbor and strode over to discuss the livestock.

"I'm going to look at the homemakers' exhibits," Mrs. Gunderson informed us. "You boys can come with me or look around here at the barns."

"We'll stay here," Acorn decided for us.

Jake strolled away to take stock of the horse teams and the show steers in their stalls.

Acorn grabbed my arm and steered me toward the midway booths. There was a man playing a trombone while a lady thumped on a piano beside him. We saw a crowd of boys and girls swarming around a booth, and when we hurried to investigate, a barker called, "Take a chance, boys, easy as pie! Just toss the ring over the bottle. Win a prize for your sweetheart!" A boy gave him a penny and threw the ring three times, but he missed them all. Acorn and I laughed and jeered along with the others before we jostled our way to another booth.

"D'you suppose Jake brought some money?" Acorn asked me.

"Not to throw away on this stuff. These are all rigged, Acorn. You can't win as easy as they make it sound."

"*I* could," he insisted.

I laughed and nudged him on down the row of carnival booths.

We met Jake and the Gundersons at the car for lunch. Later, at supper time, Mr. Gunderson bought us hamburgers and ice cream in a cone. Then Jake and Acorn and I drove home in the flivver to do the milking while Mr. and Mrs. Gunderson went to the grandstand performance. We got back to town just before dark for the dance in one of the barns.

Mr. and Mrs. Gunderson danced together. His face had relaxed into an easy grin as he swayed to the music, his arm draped around his wife's waist. Put him in a suit, he'd look almost like a city gentleman, I thought. Acorn and I wandered over to some hay bales where other kids were tussling and keeping an eye on the dancers.

I saw Helen smiling at me from the edge of the crowd of grown-ups. My ears burned as I gave her a tight little nod and then turned my back. In less than a minute, I felt a tug on my elbow and there she was. "Come and dance with me," she begged, tugging harder.

"I can't dance," I said. My heart was hammering against my rib cage.

"Yes, you can," she insisted.

Acorn laughed and shoved me from behind. I fell

toward Helen and, catching myself, found I was face to face with her. She put her hand under my elbow and pulled me out to the dance floor.

I followed her zigzagging motion across the floor as best I could, stumbling sometimes. Acorn had located some other Hawkeye boys, and they were cheering now, clapping to the music, making me feel pretty pleased with myself. Helen closed her eyes and snuggled closer. My heart gave a little flutter when her hair tickled my cheek.

I glanced back at my schoolmates, and Mollie Hannigan's eyes caught mine. She was watching me without even a trace of a smile. I felt a little stab of guilt, right away thinking how Mollie'd been the one to tell the truth about me fighting with the sticks. Then Helen leaned back and swung me around in a circle, and by the time I looked again, Mollie had disappeared.

We rode home in the dark, too tired to keep our eyes open in spite of the jolts and jerks of the flivver. Acorn and I curled up, a heap of arms and legs, in a corner of the backseat. Mrs. Gunderson's head nodded, too.

The men's voices drifted back in a soft wave of sound that lifted me up to wakefulness and dropped me back when they were quiet.

"... sold the calves to Jacobson," I heard Mr. Gunderson say.

I felt Acorn's body tense beside me.

"Good price," Mr. Gunderson went on. "He wanted all eight of 'em, but I saved out a heifer to re-place Dolly and a couple steers to butcher."

I couldn't hear Jake's response. *Sold the calves to Jacobson . . . sold the calves to Jacobson . . .* my mind kept whispering.

"We maybe should think about gettin' us one of them Fordson tractors. Jacobson sure swears by his," Mr. Gunderson's voice droned on.

Acorn didn't say a word. I told myself he must be asleep after all. I let the rhythm of the car pull me down and down, drowning out the voices of the grown-ups. Nothing—not Mollie, not anything—could ruin this perfect day for me.

Fox in the Henhouse

Something woke me in the middle of the night. I lay there in the quiet a few minutes, wondering what sound I had heard. It didn't come again.

I rolled over to go back to sleep, and that was when I realized Acorn was gone. Slinging my arm out across his side of the bed just to be sure, I felt the cool, empty sheets. Lady gave a little whine before I shushed her. I fumbled into my overalls and tiptoed across the floor with my dog at my heels.

I stopped to listen when I stepped off the porch. There was a thump from somewhere, followed by a little bleating sound. I trotted toward the barn, but the closer I got, the quieter the barn seemed to be. The cows were all out in the summer pasture.

I headed for Jake's house.

The sound came again. A grunt or a cry. Then

another thump. It was behind Jake's house . . . the henhouse!

I raced past the barn and flung the door open so hard it thudded against the wall. Acorn gave out a gasp that was part cry and swung around to face me. In the moonlight his face was ghastly white. So were the limp bodies of the chickens strewn around him.

"Acorn, what're you doing?" My words came out in a sort of groan.

His chest heaved as he struggled to catch his breath. Then he gave out a strangled, ragged kind of cry, and I realized it must have been Acorn who made the bleating sound I'd heard from the house.

I took a step toward him, but he hunched his shoulders, clenching his hands into fists, ready to fight.

I stopped.

"What are you doing to Mrs. Gunderson's chickens?" I demanded.

Acorn blinked hard, as if my question had waked him up. He reached out a hand to steady himself against the chicken roost. Suddenly I realized he was crying.

"He . . . he . . . he promised me a calf," Acorn sputtered.

I groped for some way to answer him. "No,

Acorn . . ." I started to say, but he turned away from me, letting go of the roost and standing up straight.

He sniffed hard. "Maybe it don't matter to you so much, Tree," he said. "Maybe 'cause you got Lady. It matters to me."

I couldn't think of what to say. All around him lay the grim evidence of his anger and hurt. What would Mr. Gunderson do about this? The thought made me weak, limp as the broken-necked chickens. Then I saw Acorn was watching me, sizing up what showed on my face.

Suddenly I heard a footstep behind me.

"You boys are out of bed awful early."

It was Jake.

My heart started hammering. I didn't even turn to look at him, just tucked my chin down on my chest and kind of rolled my body to the side, leaning my backbone against the doorjamb. I guess I sort of let go of my charge of Acorn—and opened the way for Jake to see the whole awful mess.

"You got something against chickens?" Jake asked my brother.

I busted out in a shaky laugh, but then I had to clamp my mouth shut because tears were squirting out the corners of my eyes.

Acorn shuffled his feet, squirming under Jake's

gaze. "I got mad," he admitted. "Sunny was mine! Mr. G went and sold *my* calf!"

Jake's eyes flicked over Acorn's face as he took in his words. "*Your* calf?" he echoed, disbelieving.

"He promised me!" Acorn cried out, unable to hold back a new gush of tears.

Jake's eyes seemed to read my brother the same way he'd read me those other times. He didn't ask more questions. Instead, he stepped past me and bent to examine the first dead chicken.

Acorn watched him, impatiently brushing the tears away, then wiping his hands on his pants. It looked like he was trying to rub away the feel of the soft feathered necks twisting and snapping under his grip.

I leaned back against the doorway, studying the two of them—Jake stroking the lifeless chickens, touching each one as if he might feel a pulse and know it hadn't happened; Acorn angry and sorry, angry and sorry. I wondered could he learn something from watching Jake that he hadn't heard in my useless explaining?

Jake sighed as his strong fingers brushed the last chicken. There were eight in all, lying broken and dead. He glanced at Acorn for just a second. Then he turned and looked at me for a long, steady moment. I saw his Adam's apple bob as he swallowed hard.

"You boys better get back to bed," he said gruffly before he stood up. "Go on," he urged as Acorn peered over at me, hesitating.

I motioned Acorn to step out ahead of me. He stumbled in a kind of daze. Something drew my eyes back to the dismal scene. I needed to tell Jake how sorry I felt. Acorn was my brother, and my feelings were as tangled and jumbled up as if I'd murdered the chickens myself.

We looked at each other in the pale light cast by the moon, and I saw the sadness on Jake's face that seemed an exact mirror of mine. I couldn't find the words I wanted, but I knew Jake understood me.

He sighed a little and dipped his head away from my gaze. "Lots of foxes out on a summer evening," he said.

I stared hard at him a minute, not sure I could believe my ears. Then I had to grin. Jake always knew how to figure a way to make things right!

Still, the worry was there as I trotted up the alleyway and followed Acorn's forlorn figure to the house. I slowed before I caught up to him. What would happen if Acorn's hotheadedness got us all in trouble—bigger trouble than even Jake could fix?

* * *

In the morning when we shuffled slowly down to breakfast, Mrs. Gunderson was heating water in her big steam boilers. On our way to the outhouse, Acorn and I saw the chickens sprawled on the grass beside the porch. Their white feathers were splotched with smatters of blood that I was sure hadn't been there the night before. Acorn shot a questioning glance at me.

"Looks like you're going to learn how to pluck a chicken," I told him.

"Funny I didn't hear that fox in the henhouse," Mrs. Gunderson muttered a few minutes later as she thumped a platter of pancakes on the table in front of us.

Acorn and I turned wide eyes on Jake.

"Yep. He was a quick one," Jake replied. He looked out the window, away from us.

"You get off a shot?" Mr. Gunderson inquired.

"Nope. He heard me and took off too quick."

"Maybe Jake and I better help you get some of them plucked before we go haying," Mr. Gunderson said to the Missus.

"The young one can do it," Jake cut in with a stern glance at Acorn.

Acorn gulped.

"I'll show him how," I offered quickly.

Mr. Gunderson eyed me sharp. I shrugged, trying to look innocent. "Unless you need me in the hay-field," I said.

"I think I can learn fast," Acorn put in, taking a cue from me.

Mr. Gunderson humphed, gave his head a shake to show he'd heard enough, and strode out the door.

"Going to make puny fryers," Mrs. Gunderson grumbled to herself as she peeked in the boilers to see was the water bubbling yet. "Such a waste!"

Jake helped us haul the boilers to the yard. I showed my brother what to do, plucking off great handfuls of feathers in a bunch, but he kept pinching little fingerfuls and then shaking the warm, wet feathers off in disgust. I was disgusted myself. Disgusted and worried over what Acorn had done. I plucked those chickens with a vengeance, outstripping my brother's slow pace.

When Mrs. Gunderson came out to help, Acorn was still mincing away at his first bird while I was starting my fourth. She bent to pick up a chicken, but I stopped her.

"I can get these," I said. "Why don't you show Acorn how to butcher them?"

Acorn glanced at me.

"Here, I'll finish your chicken," I said.

I hardly looked up as they left. I had a feeling Acorn would like pulling out the warm guts even less than plucking feathers. I hoped it made him sick. He'd earned what he was getting for turning even Jake into a liar.

At noon I offered to take lunch out to the far meadow, where Jake and Mr. Gunderson were fixing a broken axle on one of the hay wagons.

The sun was hot and I felt good, thinking maybe Acorn had learned his lesson. Swinging the lunch bucket and water pail as I walked, I whistled the way Jake did. Lady grinned and panted, trotting at my side when she wasn't trailing every fluttering bird or butterfly that winged its way past.

The field was a half mile down a worn prairie trail. I liked the way the trail buckled over the rises and dips of the land. If I could have been sure Mr. Gunderson wouldn't notice I'd have untied my boots and gone barefoot, letting the warm, fine-powdered dirt squash between my toes.

The men were hungry and thirsty. We sat down and ate in the shade of the wagon. I threw bits of bread to Lady and watched her jump to catch them.

After we ate we all lay back in the shade for a little snooze. I woke to the sound of Mr. Gunderson's voice. "I understand you love the farm," he was saying. "You know I'll have the papers set up so you'll always be able to live here if anything happens to me. It's just that I've got Gus to think of. I want him to own this place when you and I are gone."

"Gus don't have any interest in farming," Jake answered slowly.

"He's my only son," Mr. Gunderson shot back. "Maybe he wasn't cut out to be a farmer, but his roots are here. It's what our pa would have wanted."

"You think you know what Pa wanted?"

"You think I don't? You think you knew him better? Did you ever once have to go out behind the shed with him, Jake? Huh?"

There was no answer.

Mr. Gunderson spat. "Even that time the team ran away. It was me took the blame. I was oldest. I got it all, Jake. Yes, I think I knew him. I knew the flat of his hand."

"I know he was rough on you, Delton," Jake said. "He always was."

"It don't matter," Mr. Gunderson said impatiently. "He wanted me tough like him. Who'd've run this place after he was gone if he hadn't made me tough enough? And you, Jake," he went on amiably, "you've always just molded to whatever anybody else wanted. That's what's made us such good partners."

"Maybe I never knew enough to go after what I wanted."

"You never needed to. You had everything you needed right here. I been good to you, haven't I?"

It was quiet again except for the hum of a passing bee and the click-click of the dragonflies in the dry air.

"Hell, how'd we get off talkin' like this?" Mr. Gunderson snorted. "What I started to say, Jake, was I wouldn't ask you to sign anything that wasn't in your best interest. It's just some legal papers I've had drawn up about the farm."

"I like it how it is," Jake mumbled. There was an obstinate catch in his voice.

"I *said* nothing will change." Mr. Gunderson's voice cracked impatiently. "It's only a legal technicality. It would give ownership to me and Etta to protect Gus's interest if anything happened to you."

"Nobody can stop things from changing, I've learned that," said Jake. His voice was growing stronger. "And I ain't close to dying. If *you* die I'll take care of Etta and Gus just like they'd take care of me. There's nothing a paper can guarantee that an honest man's word can't vouch for better."

Mr. Gunderson spat in disgust and crawled out from under the wagon.

Jake arguing with Mr. Gunderson seemed like me talking to Acorn. Jake could no more make his brother see things his way than a jackrabbit could sprout wings and fly. They had grown as differently as if one had been planted in the shade and one in the sun. The one saw the world with eyes wide open, the other kept his eyes slitted shut. There was no way to make them look at things the same.

Match to Dry Tinder

The letter arrived the next day. It was propped on the table when we went in for supper. I sat down at my place and saw Jake catch sight of it, too, before we bowed our heads for Mrs. Gunderson's prayer.

Acorn didn't notice. He took the plate of fried chicken the Missus passed him with eyes wide and hungry. I didn't look at him when he handed me the plate. I didn't want him losing his appetite the way I'd lost mine.

Mr. Gunderson spotted the envelope, reached out, and turned it over to read the label. He glanced at the Missus. She gave her head a little shake, and he set it down again before he helped himself to mashed potatoes and peas.

I made myself take a bite. Mrs. Gunderson's fried chicken was as tasteless as lumpy oatmeal. I forced my jaws to chew, choking the food down with a swish of cool buttermilk.

After supper Mr. Gunderson leaned back in his chair and tore open the letter while Acorn and I cleared the table.

"This letter's from that Mr. Blake at the orphanage," Mr. Gunderson announced after he had scanned the page. "Just a reminder it's been a year. Says to use the voucher and send the boy back."

Jake set his elbows on the table slowly and deliberately. He leaned forward, giving Mr. Gunderson his full attention. The Missus glanced first at Jake and then at her husband. Acorn blinked, turning wide eyes to meet mine.

I looked away.

"What're you lookin' at me for?" Mr. Gunderson demanded, staring back at Jake. "The time is up. That was the deal."

Jake pivoted from the table in a slow sort of revolution that made me think of the Earth turning on its axis the way Mr. Wolverton had explained it.

"Could be," Jake said, turning his head to look straight at his brother. "Could be *your* year with him is up and now the orphanage would let *me* have a year with him, too."

Mr. Gunderson let the letter drop to his knees.

"Jake," he said, resting the palms of his hands on the table, his voice more soft and tender than I'd ever heard it, "you ain't a married man. They don't let out orphans to a bachelor."

I swallowed around a big lump in my throat. The room sort of spun before my eyes, and I bolted for the stairway. I heard Jake call out and Lady thump up the steps after me. I slammed the bedroom door, but not before she scuttled through. The sheets were cool when I threw myself down on the bed. Lady gave a little whine and shoved her cold nose against my neck. I put an arm around her to pull her close, hoping everyone, even Acorn, would stay out and leave me alone.

The kitchen was silent. They knew if they said more I'd hear it through the grate. I was glad they remembered. I didn't want to hear them discussing any part of it, as if I was already gone, a thing of their past. There was nothing to discuss anyway. Mr. Blake said I had to go back, and Jake had no say in adopting me. Acorn might stay on—Mr. Gunderson hadn't said one way or the other about him. It didn't matter. I couldn't think about Acorn now. I didn't want to think at all.

I heard Jake stride across the floor and out the door. He'd go to his house to think about it, maybe, or down to the barn. But there was no solution. I'd come one day on the train and I'd leave one day soon the same way. For the first time, I wished Mr. Blake had never picked me to go with the Gundersons.

I heard Acorn come in later, but I didn't budge, hoping he'd think I was asleep. Lady had wiggled out of my grasp and was curled up at the foot of the bed. I felt Acorn sag down beside her, and I supposed he'd wrap up with her and fall asleep.

∗ ∗ ∗

I don't know how much later I heard the noise. It sounded like Lady whining somewhere far away.

I bolted upright. The full moon shone in and I saw that Lady and Acorn were gone. How long, I wondered, had I been asleep?

I swung my legs to the floor and was surprised at the clunk they made when they hit the boards—I still had on my boots. For sure Acorn was running away without me. Now that Mr. Gunderson was sending me back, he wouldn't take the chance of being forced to return to the orphanage himself.

Somehow I had to catch him.

I tried to dash down the stairs without a sound, but my boots thumped and bumped against the steps in the dark. I heard a muffled snort from the Gundersons' bedroom as I crept clumsily though the kitchen.

Out on the porch, I heard Lady again. The sound seemed to come from down past the barn. I took off running.

Lady barked again. It was a funny sound. Close, but far. I stopped to get my bearings. A door creaked behind me, and then a thump came from over at Jake's house.

Suddenly I knew where Lady was. "Acorn!" I hollered, "Acorn, wait, I'm coming!" I sprinted down past the barn to the chicken coop, almost colliding with Jake as he stepped from the shadows by his door.

Lady sprang up to greet me as soon as I stepped into the henhouse. I caught her in my arms. The chickens turned to blink at me, fluffing their feathers and grumpily shifting on their roosts.

Acorn was nowhere in sight.

"Is it a fox?" Mr. Gunderson hollered. I saw the gleam of his shotgun barrel as he rounded the darkened corner of Jake's house.

"It's all right," I said as Lady whined and squirmed out of my arms. "It was only Lady in here. Somebody shut her in."

Jake shone a lantern into the henhouse. "Where's Acorn?" he asked.

"I'm looking for him," I called over my shoulder, taking off after Lady.

"You sure it's not a fox?" Mr. Gunderson yelled, but I didn't stop to answer. I ran past the barn and out beyond the tree rows. Lady was clean out of sight.

"Delton!" It was Mrs. Gunderson's voice, high and frightened. "Come in here! Somebody's broken my teapot! My egg money's gone!"

I stopped in my tracks, squeezing my eyes shut tight. I wished I hadn't heard what she said.

I made myself try to think. The moon was like a great lantern lighting everything. I saw the hard-packed dirt of the prairie trail glistening white like a ribbon across the land. It made sense Acorn would be headed toward that patch of willows where he'd hidden before. He knew the trail past it made a short cut to the road to Crosby and the tracks where he could hop a freight. He must have shut Lady in with the chickens thinking she'd only make trouble for him.

I heard Jake running behind me, but I took off without waiting. As I ran, Mr. Gunderson hollered back to the Missus. I didn't let myself think about the teapot or Mrs. Gunderson's money. If I was on the right trail, I should be able to catch up with Acorn pretty easily. I could run at a smooth clip with the moon as bright as it was.

I didn't stop until I came to the edge of the field. There I peered down into the little draw where light and shadow danced together the length of its grassy slopes, swallowed at the bottom by the dark patch that was the willows. I couldn't see any sign of either Lady or my brother.

"Acorn!" My voice cut loud across the quiet of the night. "Acorn, are you down there? I've got to talk to you!"

I saw a flash of white near the edge of the trees. It was Lady, darting out to glance up at me, the white fur on her neck and tail shining bright in the moon's gleam. She disappeared into the shadows again. "I see Lady!" I hollered. "I know you're down there, Acorn!"

I waited, holding my breath.

"I'm going, Tree," my brother finally answered. "Just you go on back and leave me be!"

"We're going together!" I called. "Wherever we're going, it's got to be together."

The wind whispered back to me. Jake came up behind me and stopped. We waited, listening, but Acorn didn't answer.

"Acorn!" I shouted again, "It can't hurt for us to talk!"

"Let me go alone!" Acorn's voice came out quavery but clear, as if the little night breeze wafted it like waves across water.

"Acorn, why?" I pleaded. "Let me talk to you!"

"I *got* to run!" he answered. In that instant I knew what Acorn was thinking. He'd stolen Mrs. Gunderson's egg money. He'd stolen all those jars of things he'd pretended weren't really stolen at all. He could never turn back and face the Gundersons.

"I'm coming after you," I hollered. "You wait there for me!" I shot Jake a glance and started down by myself. Jake squatted on his heels in the grass at the edge of the draw, just watching and listening, letting me handle my brother.

I wished I knew what I was going to say. What could I tell him? Nothing . . . nothing to make him turn around. But still, I had to try. I had to see him, that's what I kept thinking. I had to see him, and somehow . . .

It was then I heard Mr. Gunderson's voice at the top of the draw. "He down there?" the farmer growled. He seemed to be breathing hard from the run, and his ragged gasps floated across the night air.

"He's in the willows," Jake answered softly.

I pushed forward, partly in the shadows of the draw, partly in the clear moonlight. I hoped Acorn was watching and saw that I was coming alone. I had a bad feeling about what Acorn would think when he heard Mr. Gunderson's voice.

"Where are you, Acorn?" I called. He didn't answer, but Lady let out a whine, and I thought I might have heard Acorn shush her.

"He's over there!" Mr. Gunderson hollered. At the bottom of the slope, I stopped and spun around to glare at him, feeling the mad rising in my chest. I wished he'd see this was between my brother and me and keep out of it. Mr. Gunderson had walked away from Jake along the edge of the draw, trying to get a glimpse of Acorn, and it surprised me that I could see him so clearly in the moonlight that I could even make out the stripes on his overalls. He stood staring intently at a spot to my left where he must have seen a movement in the willows. He clutched his shotgun as if he expected to flush out a fox, after all.

There was the slap of a willow branch and I knew Acorn must be running again. "Acorn, wait!" I shouted, running, too.

Suddenly the roar of the shotgun shattered the night air. From the corner of my eye I saw the tongue of flame as Mr. Gunderson fired off a warning shot.

"Come out of there!" he yelled. "You little thievin' rascal! You can't get away from us!"

All I could think was that Acorn would panic now. I had to get to him.

A branch cracked, and I made out a flash of movement at the edge of the thicket. In the next instant my heart seemed to stop beating. I was sure I saw moonlight glinting off something long and shiny. It looked like the muzzle of a rifle, poking out from between the willow branches!

"Acorn!" I tried to shout again, but my throat had closed up tight.

There was a rustle and a scrape behind me, and I knew without turning that Jake was scrambling down the draw. I plunged ahead.

"Where are you? Come out here!" Mr. Gunderson shouted. Maybe because of the shadows in the thicket, he hadn't seen the rifle.

I didn't break stride. Below me I saw the gun barrel wobble as my brother struggled to steady the stock against his shoulder. I saw his finger finding its place on the trigger, his hands trembling. All I had to do was knock the gun out of his hands.

Behind me came the sound of Jake's boots scuffing, and then a grunt as he stumbled and went down on the uneven slope.

Acorn gave a startled jerk and swung the gun wildly toward the noise.

"Acorn! No!" I screamed. "No!"

I lunged hard, flinging myself between Jake and the rifle.

There was a roar in my ears just before the bullet hit. Fire exploded across my skull, flaring like a match struck and touched to dry tinder. Red flames shot through my eyes, blinding me, and I reeled under the sharp, crackling pain.

I pitched forward, my knees buckling and sending me face first into the grass. I heard Jake running again before he slid to a stop beside me. He grabbed my shoulder, rolling me over.

"Oh, Tree, no! Oh, Tree!" Acorn cried, choking and sobbing as he scrambled out of the willows.

I tried to grasp a breath to answer him, but darkness closed me in.

After the Fire

The barn was on fire. Red and yellow flames shot up, devouring the tinder-dry walls. There was a BOOM! and I whirled to the right. A fiery beam collapsed, peppering the sky with a cascade of sparks as it crashed to the ground. More flaming barns reared up out of the earth. To the left! Then to the right! Dry heat seared my face and scorched my laboring lungs. I was choking in the smoke. Throwing up my arms, I ran, terrified, as another barn exploded behind me.

"Has he woken up yet?" a voice said—Mr. Gunderson. Someone grunted an answer before he spoke again. "Doc should be back again soon to check on him."

A warm wave washed over me, pulling me back to the world of burning barns.

"Seems to be sleeping peaceably enough." Mr. Gunderson's voice was closer, jarring me awake again.

"Doc said you did the right thing to come get him. Said the kid would have bled to death on the ride to town."

"He's still lost a lot of blood." This from Jake.

"I'll keep the other boy with me." Now Mr. Gunderson seemed to be moving away. "We got plenty of chores to do—we'll check the binder and get down the canvas. Don't see as how I can trust him out of my sight."

"You talk to him?"

"Talked with a rod. Gave him a few good switches. I thought about breakin' his fingers. Geez, Jake, what would make a couple of worthless kids think they can rifle through other people's houses and come out shootin' a man's own gun?"

Jake didn't answer. The only sound was the clump and shuffle of boots on the floor. I knew where I was now. I knew the smells: Jake's bedding and the soft scent of kerosene that lingered even during the day when the lamp was out.

Mr. Gunderson swore. "Here it is almost harvest and I got one kid laid up and one I can't trust enough to turn my back on. I knew that Blake fellow had it in for me."

"Things are never simple."

Mr. Gunderson snorted. "I have a good notion to put the young one on the train this afternoon. Wouldn't you know, just when we need him the most, he pulls a fool trick like this! Here I've kept them all this time thinkin' they'd be useful, finally."

"Let's wait until the doc comes back. We ought to all talk before we do anything."

"Leastwise I locked my guns up where no one can get at 'em. You better keep a close eye on yours, too, Jake."

The door slammed, making my head throb.

I heard Jake cross the floor as he came to stand over my bed. Slowly, painfully, I opened my eyes. His frown softened to a smile when he saw I was awake.

"Hello," he said. "You finally coming to?"

I started to sit up, but a pain flashed through my head and I sank back down.

"Better stay still," Jake advised. "The doctor's coming by soon to have another look at you."

"It's morning?"

"Yeah, it's morning. And you've had one long night of it."

"What . . . what happened?"

"Bullet sliced its way across the side of your head. Good thing you got a thick skull. Doc thinks you'll get by without too much more damage than a rough haircut and a bad headache." Jake chuckled at his own joke.

I started to smile, but immediately sobered as pain stabbed me again. "Where's Acorn?" I asked.

Jake's smile turned down. "He's out helping Delton."

"I should talk to him."

"He knows you're all right." Jake set his lips tight.

"Jake," I pleaded, "you can't let Mr. Gunderson send Acorn back without me."

"Acorn is too much for any of us to handle," Jake stated firmly. "He don't belong here. He was all set to run away anyhow." I supposed Jake had found Acorn's stash of jars out there in the willow trees.

"He doesn't really want to leave—he's just dead set against going back to the orphanage. Please don't let my brother go back there, Jake."

"Your brother," he said, his eyes piercing mine as though he were searching for something deeper. "You think this brotherhood thing is really that important?"

"Important?"

"A brother ain't yourself. Maybe you got to separate you from him sometimes. So you both survive."

He was bargaining with me some way that I didn't understand.

"Acorn ain't got no one but me, Jake," I reminded him.

Jake studied me for another long minute. Then he sighed. I knew he wished I'd said something different. I watched as he set his jaw, as though he'd taken one defeat and now he had to face the next battle.

"Acorn had quite an arsenal of supplies ready for running away," he said. It was an accusation.

I blushed, blazing hot. Red. The color of guilt—the color of shame. If I could have wished it into being, I'd have wished my old gray color back.

"Yes," I muttered low.

"You knew." It wasn't a question. He had only been waiting to hear me admit it.

I couldn't answer. My stomach started boiling and my head pounded harder.

"He tell you he planned to take the money?" Jake asked suddenly. His voice was quiet and tired. I couldn't bear it. And I couldn't cover for Acorn. Not to Jake.

"He told me," I admitted. I had to stop and wait for the pain to settle down, shutting my eyes and trying to breathe easy. Then I made myself open my eyes and look at Jake. "Acorn had a lot of plans. I let his stashing stuff go, but I thought I'd . . . well, I *hoped* I'd talked him out of robbing anybody."

Our eyes locked as Jake absorbed my words. I could smell him, that solid sweat that was Jake's, blending with the familiar scents of his house.

"He said you knew he planned to run away," Jake said slowly. "But what about the gun?"

"He didn't plan to hurt anybody, Jake." My voice came out shaky. It was hard to hold back the tears. "I don't . . . I guess Acorn thought he needed the gun to survive out on the land." I heard myself begging for him to understand. "I tried to make him change his mind. I hoped . . . I hoped he'd come to *see* . . ."

I tore my eyes away, blinking hard.

Jake stood up and strode over to the window. "We can't—a boy that's a murderer . . . We can't keep him here."

The heat flared up inside me again. "He ain't no murderer, Jake! He panicked when Mr. Gunderson fired his gun. No one was murdered. I don't think he—"

"*You* were the next thing to murdered," Jake flung at me, swinging around to face me again.

"But I ain't dead, Jake! I ain't!" I struggled up to sway dizzily on the edge of the bed. "Thanks to you, who wouldn't let me bleed to death. Thanks to you, he ain't no murderer. You saved us both!" I fought the pesky tears and my roaring head, trying to hold his blazing gaze.

There was a knock on the door, and a man swung it open. He stood for a moment, clutching a black bag and blinking at me and then over at Jake.

"Doc . . ." Jake began.

"Lie down, lie down," the doctor said to me, shooting Jake an angry glare. "I told you to keep him quiet!"

I did as I was told.

"How's the head?" I heard the doctor ask me as he pressed my eyelids back and peered into my eyes.

"Hurts," I whispered, hoping Jake couldn't hear. "A lot."

✳ ✳ ✳

My head still throbbed when Jake brought supper, but I pulled myself up to a sitting position as he plumped a pillow behind my back. He laid a board across my knees and pulled the cover off a bowl of thick, creamy potato soup. Acorn shuffled in behind Jake, carrying his own soup and a basket of Mrs. Gunderson's buttered buns. He glanced at me before he set his bowl on the table.

Jake muttered something about going up to the house for supper and left us alone. Acorn sat down gingerly on one of the chairs. Neither of us spoke.

I spooned in a few bites of the soup before I leaned back on my pillow and cradled my head in my hands. Acorn scraped his bowl clean, set his spoon down, and trundled over to perch carefully at the foot of the cot. "How's your head?" he asked.

"Sore," I said.

"I thought I'd killed you."

I grunted, sliding the board to one side and easing my head back down on the pillow.

"Think I'll go to jail?" Acorn asked.

I considered, fumbling through the maze of pain in my head. "No," I said. "I ain't dead, Acorn."

"You looked dead," he said accusingly. As if it were my fault for scaring him nearly to death. It made me mad.

"Could have *been* dead just as easy," I retorted. "You had no business shooting that gun, Acorn."

"I didn't mean to shoot anybody!"

"You had your finger on the trigger," I snapped, cold as ice.

"But Mr. Gunderson was shooting at *me*," Acorn countered. He dropped his eyes. "Or at least I thought he was. All I could think was I *couldn't* go back—and you were dead set against living out on our own!" He stopped and ducked his chin to his chest as though he knew it was pointless to go over it all again.

When he raised his head, his eyes were different. Sad, I guess. Sorry. "I was wrong, Tree, I see that now," he said softly. "I saw you layin' there. And Jake—I wished . . . oh . . . I wished I could of broke the gun and run as far as I could. Only—only I couldn't think where to go. With you layin' there."

Acorn paused and picked at a yarn tie poking through the quilting stitches. His eyes were dry. His face was listless, as if he were too miserable, too hopeless to cry. I wanted to shake him and I wanted to hug him at the same time. Acorn surely had a talent for making bad things worse.

"I know they'll send me back," he stated flatly, as if he were reporting the weather. "It don't matter to me anymore."

His words bothered me. He wasn't saying *we'd* have to go back. It was only him. As if he'd killed our brotherhood with the bullet. "Acorn," I said, softening, "I know you didn't mean to shoot me. I know that."

He looked at me hopefully and gave a little sniff. "Tree," he said, his voice quavering, "all I could think about today when I got the whippin' and all the time after, even when I apologized to Mrs. G, was how you did that for Jake. How you knew I was gonna pull the trigger, and you jumped out to take the bullet for Jake. I thought about that all day.

"Then tonight when Jake said we could bring you supper and I knew for sure you were going to be all right, I got a new thought. You did it for me, too, didn't you? You knew it would go better for me shootin' just an orphan than shootin' either Jake or Mr. G. I wish I could think fast like you, Tree. I wish I could see things the way you do."

I stretched out my arms for him then, and he tumbled forward and buried his head in my chest. We hung on to each other, me with my aching head, him with his aching butt. We cried like two lost brothers who'd found each other again.

The Hardest Bargain

If someone asked me if it was worth it to get shot to make Acorn come around to seeing things differently, I'd have had to say yes. The fire of the setting sun was still streaming in Jake's windows when Acorn and I got done with our peacemaking. It might have been the angles of shadow and light from the lay of Jake's house, but I thought, as I looked at Acorn, that his brown eyes and blotches of freckles and rosy cheeks looked as though someone had painted them there, the way Leroy Johnson's face looked when I first went to Hawkeye School.

"I brought you somethin'," Acorn said, kind of quiet. I watched as he pulled a dirty cloth out of his shirt. He unfolded it carefully to reveal his knife. We both sat still for a moment, admiring the carved handle and the heavy blade.

"Finest thing I ever owned," Acorn crooned. He

rubbed his thumb across the edge, just to check if it still felt sharp.

Then he looked at me with a shy smile. "I want you to keep it," he said. "It'll only get me in trouble back at the orphanage. And you can maybe find some use for it." I started to speak, but he stopped me with a somber look that I knew from experience meant I was to let him finish.

"I'm going back, Tree," he said. "Mr. Gunderson is going to send me anyway, and I don't blame him for being mad. I'm going back so Jake can find a way to keep you. It's me Gunderson wants as far away as a ticket will take me."

I shook my head, stumbling over what to say, but Acorn ignored me and went on talking. "I'll do just like you did," he said. "I'll put up with things at the orphanage as long as it takes and maybe get sent out to a farm. I can handle it. I can be my own self just like you are." I know I was staring at him, trying to take in the changes that had come over him since he fired Gunderson's rifle.

Before I could answer, there was a thump, and Jake pushed open the door and came in. He stopped and took in the sight of us, his clear blue eyes coming to rest on the shining knife in Acorn's hand. His gaze shot up to mine, flaming with questions.

"I brought him my knife," Acorn quickly volunteered. "I want him to keep it for me."

Jake lifted his eyebrows, wrinkling his broad forehead, as he narrowed his eyes skeptically at Acorn. "Then give it to him," he said. His voice was cold, the closest to his own brother's voice as I'd ever heard it.

Acorn hastily glanced at me, shame clouding his face. He laid the knife beside me on the cot and stood up uncertainly.

Jake's boots were loud on the board floor as he strode over to the water pitcher. He filled the basin and rolled back his sleeves, lathering his hands with soap. "You take these dishes up to the Missus now," he ordered, cocking a stern eye at Acorn. "And help her wash 'em up."

"Yes, sir," Acorn croaked hoarsely. He bolted across the floor, past Jake, and out the door.

Jake let his eyes light on mine as he finished scrubbing. They were dark blue, like the sky in the west when a storm is brewing. I waited for him to say what he was thinking.

"You gave the knife back to him?" he asked, steely-eyed as Mr. Gunderson.

"It's—he's—it's his knife," I stammered, swallowing hard. "He was just telling me how scared he got after he shot the gun."

"Should scare him," Jake said. He pulled out a chair and slumped heavily into it.

"He was alone against all of us. He wasn't thinking," I said. My voice sounded desperate, even to me.

"You shouldn't feel you have to defend him, boy. He'll only bring you trouble. . . . You had a life here without him!"

My mouth fell open as I stared at Jake. I knew what he was saying. Jake would find a way for me . . . except, never with Acorn.

Every part of me ached.

"I can't. I can't stay here without my brother," I whispered, because my voice wouldn't come out any louder. "He told me he knows he was wrong all along. And he wants to try to see things like I do, Jake. He wants to try." I swallowed hard to keep myself from blubbering like a baby. "I can't let him go off without me."

"He's lucky to have you, boy," Jake said. His voice sounded as if it came from somewhere far away. He frowned, thinking hard, before he pushed back his chair and stood up.

I made myself watch him stride purposefully to the door.

"Jake," I said, slinging out the name like a lasso to stop him. He paused, half turning his head, his hand on the knob. "Nobody ever done for me what you done," I said. "I can't . . . I can't ever forget that. Thank you for standing up for me. And for Acorn." It wasn't enough to say, but it was all I could get out.

Jake didn't look at me. He nodded, listening, his eyes on the floor. He nodded again, pressing his lips together hard.

Then he was gone.

I think the hardest sound I ever heard was Jake closing that door behind him. I felt as though a mighty hand had reached down inside me and torn everything soft clean out. Like that barn I saw the first day I came here. No one could have told me one day I'd have to be strong enough to say no to Jake Gunderson. I wouldn't have done it, either, for anyone less than my brother.

That's what my choice came down to. But I'd had to face hard bargains before. And I knew there was one thing I wouldn't do wrong again. I wouldn't give up what family I already had—my own brother—to make myself any kind of new family without him.

Someone to Die For

I heard Jake come in that night, late. He didn't light the lamp, just moved around as quietly as he could, rolling out the bedding on my old place on the floor. I didn't sleep much, there were so many things on my mind, but I must have dozed toward morning, because when I opened my eyes the sun was up. I thought Jake would already be letting the milk cows in, but to my surprise he was sitting on a chair, one boot pulled on, his eyes lost somewhere in the sky outside the window.

I didn't make a sound, just watched him. When he recollected himself and picked up the other boot, he moved in a sort of fog, as if his mind wasn't focused on getting out to the barn at all.

When he left I dressed myself, and when I heard Acorn and the men carrying the full milk pails to the kitchen cellar, I plodded up to meet them for breakfast.

I was determined to make myself useful, even though Mrs. Gunderson had stopped by before bedtime to check on me and vouch she'd send meals as long as I felt poorly. Jake followed me in the kitchen door, but I couldn't find it in me to look at him. Acorn shot me a quick grin to show he was glad I was up and around, but even he seemed to be in a quiet mood.

Mrs. Gunderson raised her eyebrows and flashed me a quick smile as she set out bowls and spoons.

"I've come to a decision," Mr. Gunderson announced as soon as we'd all sat down. "Not an easy one, but one I can live with. I'm sendin' you boys back on the train first of next week."

Acorn's eyes skipped to me and I gave my head a little shake, meaning not to worry for me. There hadn't been time to tell him I wouldn't stay without him.

"Looks like you'll be well enough to travel," Mr. Gunderson said to me before he let his glance flick to Acorn. "I got a harvest to think about and I don't want to have to be watchin' my back wonderin' what some hell-bent kid is up to. That's the way it'll be."

Mrs. Gunderson pursed her lips and glanced at each of us without meeting our eyes. Jake squared his shoulders and sucked in a deep breath. Then he pushed back his bowl.

"I can't let you do that, Delton," he declared, crossing his arms over his chest. I stared at him, a flicker of hope rising in my heart and a shadow of despair tramping it down at the same time. "This boy saved my life."

"Your life wouldn't have been in danger if these orphans hadn't been here," Mr. Gunderson shot back hotly. "They could have killed us all!"

"The boy jumped in front of the gun to save me. I can't let you send him back."

"You can't keep him, Jake. We've already discussed this. You can't let foolish sentiment . . . a fluke of fate . . . get in the way of concern for your own family."

"Someone who's ready to die for you *is* family," Jake asserted, quiet and simple.

Mr. Gunderson opened his mouth to reply, but no sound came out. I stopped breathing. It seemed to me even the bird sounds and the wind's whispers were hushed, listening. Acorn's eyes were glued to Jake's face.

"Jake, listen to yourself," Mr. Gunderson pleaded. "*Family?* You've let this boy get to you. We only brought him for a year."

Jake made no response. It was as if his last statement stood without need of defense or embellishment.

"Jake," his brother said, louder. "I can't keep a murderer on the place. You fight the orphanage, then, if you really want to keep this boy. But I won't let the young one stay."

Jake's eyes made a sweep of my face. I met his look without blinking.

He turned back to his brother. "The boy ain't no murderer, Delton," Jake declared, my words echoing in his as clear as a ringing bell. "No one was murdered. It was an accident. A scared kid pulling a trigger in a panic. Your gun was the first one fired."

"I fired a warning shot to stop him!" Mr. Gunderson snapped back. "He was running off with Etta's money."

"He was running from a place he'd never been welcome at. Running in a panic. The stealing was wrong—I'm not saying he don't have to make it right."

My spoon slipped from my hand with a clatter. Acorn stared up, speechless, at Jake.

"We need a hired man," Jake continued, keeping his eyes fastened on his brother's. "I say we hire the boy. He's finished eighth grade. He's old enough to do a man's job."

"*Hire* him!" Mr. Gunderson roared.

"And let the younger boy be *his* responsibility,"

Jake continued. "He only needs a little more size, a little more time and direction. This is a better place for him to grow up than off in some city orphanage."

"You've lost your marbles, Jake!" Mr. Gunderson thundered. "They go back, like I said. Should have shipped 'em out six months ago."

"Then I go with them."

A lump swelled up in my throat so it hurt to swallow. Mr. Gunderson's jaw hung slack as he stared at his brother. "What are you sayin'?" he asked, as if he'd had the wind kicked out of him.

"That I'll go to St. Paul and talk to the man at the orphanage. Tell him what's happened here this year. Remind him the boy is thirteen and old enough to decide himself who he wants to adopt him. We'll find a job. Work side by side. Like father and son. And sons."

"You really mean this?" Mr. Gunderson breathed, caving back into his chair like a collapsing tent. "You'd leave me? Leave your home?"

Jake dropped his eyes, bent his head. I read his silence as clear as a printed page. Mr. Gunderson did, too. "You'd leave me alone for the harvest!" His voice gained a little ground, spurred by disbelief.

"You give me no choice," Jake stated softly.

"I'm your brother, Jake," Mr. Gunderson reminded him. "I've always looked out for you."

"And you'll always be my brother. But you've never needed me like this boy does. Only for the harvest. Only for the farm. That's the way you need me.

"I never saw nothing braver than what he done the other night. Nothing simpler. He stepped out and did what he had to do—I see it now. He showed me something I've tried to figure how to do all my life. So today I stand up and do what I have to do, the same way."

Silence seemed to pin each of us in his place. Outside I heard the wind pick up, just the smallest sound.

After what seemed a long while, I noticed Mrs. Gunderson's fingers, clutching and unclutching the arm of her chair. As if she were making ready to flee and then pulling herself back again, holding herself in. Tears rolled unchecked down her pudgy cheeks. Her eyes were focused somewhere far away, maybe on Fargo and Gus.

"Then it will have to be the way you say, Jake," Mr. Gunderson said gruffly. "You've backed me into a hard place." His words plowed a furrow through the silence. "We will have a hired man, then. And his brother."

Mr. Gunderson stood up and fixed his eyes like

hawk's talons on Acorn. "But I am still the man in charge here. You will do as I say, not a step out of line, or I'll be damned if I don't run you clean off the place. And you'll pay back double in work for that money you stole from my wife. You understand what I'm telling you?"

Acorn nodded vigorously.

Jake smiled at Acorn's nodding head.

Then his eyes met mine. I couldn't keep my chin from quivering, though I pressed my lips tight between my teeth. My eyes were misting over with tears, but I held his gaze. "Like father and son," he'd said. I'd heard it with my own ears, saw it now in his clear blue eyes.

Jake shoved back his chair and stood up.

I found myself running clumsily across the kitchen floor to throw my arms around his strong, hard shoulders.

He wrapped his arms around me, too. His strength felt like a power going right through to the heart of me. My mind flashed back to the first day I'd come here, to the fire and the wind and all the powers that had worked such hard bargains with me. None of it mattered now.

We had a place—me and Acorn. And all because

of Jake. He'd seen the best in me, I guess. Colors, maybe, that I never knew were there. Whatever it was he saw, he'd opened wide a door.

I'd come home.

Epilogue

After harvest Jake did take Acorn and me back to St. Paul to talk to Mr. Blake about all that had happened that year. Mr. Blake agreed that under the circumstances, and being we were brothers and as old as we were, we could be adopted by a bachelor if we all saw fit.

I started high school in Crosby that fall. Jake said that even if I was the hired man, I needed my education. My studies were going well. Mollie Hannigan was my study partner in algebra, my hardest subject. She had a way of explaining problems I couldn't get, just keeping at it until I saw it right.

When hunting season came, Jake told Acorn he ought to use his knife for gutting and skinning the deer we brought in. Then he let Acorn hang the knife on the wall with his rifle, and it gleamed down at us as if it belonged there.

About a month after we got back from St. Paul, a package arrived for Jake. It was wrapped in brown paper and looked mighty interesting, but in spite of our curious glances Jake didn't open it.

He was late coming down to do the milking that evening. After supper he sat quietly reading while Acorn and I did our schoolwork at the little table. The light from the kerosene lantern cast sparkles of yellow and orange against the walls. I looked around, as I often did when we were all quiet, thinking how warm and safe that house, that room, always felt.

After Acorn and I closed our books that night, trooped to the outhouse, and washed at the basin, we opened the door to our bedroom. Jake had added a room for us onto his house after the grain was hauled in the fall. Acorn was the first one in, and he stopped so sudden I nearly ran him over.

Hanging over the head of our beds were two signs that reminded me of the white paper names I'd nailed over the cows' mangers so long ago.

TREE
Theodore Jacob Gunderson

ACORN
Alexander Jacob Gunderson

Smith was the only name in our files at the orphanage. But Acorn and I both preferred Gunderson—Jacob Gunderson. A name, I always thought, should link a person to his beginnings.